Sharing the Itty-Bitty Vixen

5 Hot-Wife Sharing Stories

Lacey Cross

Twisted Rose Publishing

Contents

Preface

These stories are arranged chronologically based on Jessica's experiences, even though I wrote them out of sequence. When you come across the two erotic shorts titled 'Sharing His Eager Hotwife', treat those as a sexy little break from the longer stories. Enjoy!

Sharing His Adventurous Wife

Chapter 1

The sound of kids running around and laughing wakes me up. I blink at the harsh light filtering through the air vent on the roof of our tent. It's already stifling in here, and the day has barely begun. I'm so **not** the camping type, and this isn't my preferred way to wake up. Give me a big soft bed in a fancy hotel with a spa to pamper me, please.

Why did I come on this trip again? I smirk when my pussy buzzes. Oh, yeah, my wonderful husband claims he has plans and this will be fun. Ms. Kitty believes him, so it better be worth it.

Recently I found a bunch of slutty hotwife porn in my husband's browser history, and he admitted he gets off on the idea of me fucking other guys. Even though Lucas is worth never having another guy's cock inside of me, I have always wrestled with the idea of monogamy. I'd never cheat on him, but before we said "I do," I gave deep thought to our marriage vows. I didn't think I'd ever meet someone who could rein in my slutty side or be able to satisfy my high sex drive, but I found the perfect guy for me.

My marriage is pretty awesome.

And finding out my husband was masturbating while imagining me with other guys? That was fucking hot.

After he admitted to his filthy desires, we banged like rabbits on every surface in the house for days while I kept a running fantasy in my head. I kept thinking I was fucking different guys while Lucas watched.

Yeah, that was a *wonderful* week.

Eventually, we had a heart-to-heart chat about what he really wanted. He asked if I would consider being a hotwife. Ms. Kitty started fluttering and tingling, like she was getting ready to train for a marathon of cocks, but my brain was more cautious than my slutty pussy. I told Lucas I'd consider it, but I wanted to take it slow.

Which, I guess, is why we're here. He's got something planned, but I don't know about this. I don't *need* to be a hotwife. What if it ruins our marriage? Sure, the idea sounds amazing, but how good can it really be? It's not like Lucas sucks in bed. I'm incredibly satisfied. He knows exactly what I like, and there's none of that awkward first-date-sex bullshit.

Where is Lucas anyway?

I sit up and stretch. My sleeping bag falls, exposing my naked breasts to the warm air. There is one positive about camping: it puts Lucas in a kinky mood. We zipped our sleeping bags together last night, and he fucked me so thoroughly he had to put his hand over my mouth to muffle my screams. I woke up wet, and thinking about how hard I came makes me want to find Lucas and ride him before I shower. We'll get nice and dirty before we get clean.

The sound of the zipper on the tent flap breaks through my slutty daydream, and I pull the edge of the sleeping bag up to cover my breasts out of caution. When the door opens, the familiar sight of my hubby makes me let go of the edge of the bedding so he can get an eyeful. I only have to flash my boobs at him, and he's putty in my hands.

Hey, wait. His hair is wet, and he's carrying a towel. Well shit, there goes my plan. He's already showered.

He blows me a kiss. "Good morning, baby. I think it's safe for you to hit the showers. Most of the kids and parents left. I only saw a bunch of guys."

His words and a lusty twinkle in his eyes perks Ms. Kitty up. Um... he's not thinking I'm going to do anything with another guy, is he?

I keep my voice light and teasing. "Since there are separate bathrooms for the men and the women, I doubt I'll be showering with a bunch of guys."

Mmm. I don't hate the idea. All those soapy hands running up and down my body, making sure they get every crack and cranny clean? Okay, focus Jessica. Your life isn't one of the reverse harem books you write.

My stomach hardens at the thought of the latest story I'm writing, and I try to push aside my concern. I've got a half-edited draft waiting for me at home, but Lucas and I need this break. My book and my readers will have to be patient.

It's actually amazing to me. People wait for my books. A couple of years ago, I got brave and published a vampire reverse harem series, and it took off. It's still difficult to wrap my head around the fact that people want to read the dirty stories that rattled around in my head all my life. I'm making enough money writing that I hired my best friend, Miri, to work as my personal assistant. Miri told me to enjoy a long weekend because there's nothing that has to be done right this second. So I went, and that's what I'm going to do.

So, yeah... chill the fuck out, brain. We're here to relax and fuck our sexy husband.

A low hum of desire rumbles through me as I watch Lucas put down his shower supplies. He's tall enough he can't stand up inside the tent, and he's moving around in a crouch.

I definitely don't have that problem. I like to claim I'm five feet, one inch tall, but that's if I stretch my spine. I'm really only five feet tall, but only me and my doctor know the truth. Not that the one inch matters, but I was teased growing up for being so tiny, so I always lie about my height. Spiked high heels give me a nice lift, and I enjoy being short. I have fun pretending to be helpless when I can't reach the top shelf in the kitchen. Lucas *has to* come in and get things down for me, and then I always give him a proper reward.

Yeah, I've got sex on the brain this morning. I clearly need an orgasm. It's got to be a rule for vacation, right? Orgasms every day!

Lucas keeps glancing at me, and I can tell his devious brain is churning over something. God, I hope it's sexual. Starting the day relaxed after another orgasm is perfect.

Once he's done puttering around, he lowers himself to the ground and crawls over me. He pushes me onto my back and gives me a deep kiss. Mmm, now this is more like it.

I wrap my arms around his neck and pull him to me. My nipples harden as he coaxes my lips open and slides his tongue inside, twining it with mine. I try to grind against him, but the puffy sleeping bag is too thick. Dammit, this isn't going to work.

With his hands on either side of my head, Lucas pulls away from the kiss and looks down at me, murmuring, "You're so fucking sexy."

I'm sure my long blonde hair is a mess, and I've got morning breath, but if he thinks I'm sexy, who am I to argue?

I smile at him and rub my legs together. "Why don't you take your clothes off and we can continue where we left off last night?"

He brings a hand up to my breast and plays with the nipple, tweaking it gently and making me gasp. When he doesn't immediately respond, I assume I've won. Hell yeah, Ms. Kitty is going to get another workout.

His eyes deepen with lust as he continues to pull on the stiff peak. "Oh, I've got a better idea."

Pleasure shoots from my breast downwards and I moan. "Mmm, yes?"

My eyes drift closed as I enjoy the delicious sensations his nimble fingers create deep in my core. I'm down with whatever plan he's cooked up, as long as he keeps his hands on me. He moves down to suck on the opposite nipple and the pleasure sets my mind adrift.

He mumbles around my tit. "Baby, I've got a challenge for you."

What's this? I crack my eyes open and run my fingers through his hair, tugging gently so he raises his head from my breast.

"Challenge? Whaddya mean?"

I'm still mentally fuzzy and not paying attention to anything but his hand on my other breast. I'm desperate to get his cock inside me, so I'll do whatever he asks as long as we can fuck afterwards.

"It's your first official hotwife challenge."

I stop running my fingers through his hair and stare at him. "Official what?"

What is he talking about? What's a hotwife challenge? We've only talked about dipping our toes into this area. I'm not sure I'm up for a challenge of any sort.

My body heats, and I grow even wetter when his lips twitch deviously. He says, "The shower rooms have a row of windows with blinds. I want you to open the blinds and leave the shower curtain open while you're in there."

That's it? That's the challenge? Easy enough. What are the chances someone is going to walk by?

I pretend to think about it. "Hmm.... What's my reward for doing this?"

He laughs. "That depends on you. We'll discuss the reward when you get back."

I arch an eyebrow at him and give it one second of consideration. "Okay. I'll do it."

No problem. I can take a quick shower and when I choose my reward, I'll tell him I want his cock.

I push him off of me and climb out of the sleeping bag, wiggling my naked ass in his direction as I dig through my duffle bag for clothes. It's not far away, so I toss on some tiny jean shorts and a t-shirt before grabbing my shower supplies.

I wink at him as I leave. "See you soon for my reward!"

He laughs. "Have fun, baby."

The park is quiet as I walk to the central bathrooms. I think he's right. Most of the families are off on their day adventure. The women's bathroom is deserted, and I put my stuff down on a wooden bench before opening the blinds in front of the shower stall.

Oh shit, people *can* see straight in here. Calm down. I mean, really, what are the chances? If it happens, which I doubt, it'll most likely be a woman coming to take a shower, anyway.

As I take my clothes off, I peek outside the window and scan the park. My pussy clenches as I imagine a stranger walking past. It's been years since anyone but Lucas or spa professionals have seen me naked.

This is more erotic than I expected.

The shower requires quarters if I want warm water. Since I don't plan on being here long, I don't need to give it many. As I step under the warm spray, a twinge of vulnerability makes me consider closing the curtain, but I brush it aside. No, this is the challenge, and I want Lucas's cock.

I keep it open and quickly soap myself up while eyeing the window. Every second that goes by without someone walking past turns me on even more. I give my shaved pussy more attention than is necessary, slipping a finger between my folds to rub my clit. Pings of bliss ripple through me and I bite back a moan. Why is this turning me on?

A thought stills my hand. Oh, holy fuck, I want a guy to see me naked.

My entire body lights up and I release my moan this time. I'm petite, blonde, and I have big breasts. I know I'm sexy, and the thought of someone other than my husband seeing me and possibly enjoying the view is so fucking hot.

Lucas might know me better than I know myself.

I lean against the shower wall and work my fingers on my clit. I imagine Lucas sending a guy into the shower to fuck me, and my legs quiver as I race towards my orgasm. Little gasps of pleasure escape my lips. Just when I'm about to close my eyes and let the bliss overtake me, movement outside the window catches my attention.

A guy and a woman walk past, chatting. The woman doesn't look this way, but the guy does. His eyes meet mine and I freeze with my hand between my legs. He gives me a wide smile. Before I can react, they walk out of view.

Ohhhh, my god.

I work my hand furiously against my clit, oblivious to anything but my pleasure. In moments, I'm on the edge. When my orgasm hits, it's so hard I cry out. I buck my hips as waves of delight rush through me and my mind blanks.

I'm panting as I come down, and a sudden blast of cold water shocks me back to my senses.

Fuck!

I squeal and step out of the shower before feeding in another quarter so I can rinse off. I want to make sure Ms. Kitty is clean again.

My brain is mush from the intense orgasm, and I rush through drying off and stalk towards my tent and my husband. I don't know what reward he's going to offer me. I almost feel like I already got rewarded, but I'm curious to see what he says.

He's sitting cross-legged on our bed, waiting for me with a shit-eating grin on his face. A glance at his crotch reveals he's hard. I drop my stuff and launch myself at him. He laughs and lies down so I'm on top of him as I ravish his mouth. I grind against his hardness, and Ms. Kitty makes it abundantly clear she wants more than my fingers this time.

Between deep kisses, I ask my question. "So what's my reward?"

He chuckles and pulls me down for another toe-curling kiss before answering. "You'll see later."

I fumble with his pants, desperate to get his cock out. His answer frustrates me, but also turns me on even more.

Yeah, this trip got a lot more interesting.

Chapter 2

Something tickles my nose and wakes me up. My eyes are still closed and I brush it away from me in my groggy state. When it comes back again, I crack my eyes open. Lucas is lying on his side next to me. He's holding a feather he found in the grass while we were setting up our tent. My first instinct it to tell him to stop touching my nose with a filthy feather, but his adorable grin melts my heart.

I stretch and yawn. "Did we sleep long?"

After masturbating in the shower, I came back to the tent and rode Lucas until we were both exhausted and had to nap.

"Not too long, but I still want to take that nature hike. We need to go before it gets any later."

Bleh. Doesn't he understand I'm a city girl and don't go hiking? He claims this is a walk along a scenic path through the woods and isn't really a hike. He also promised I'd see pretty flowers, and I'm a sucker for flowers, so I guess it'll be fun.

I unzip the sleeping bag and kick it down. "Okay, let's do this."

As I crawl to the end of the tent and dig around in my bag for clothes to wear, Lucas paws through the bag next to him.

"Jessica, I want you to wear this."

Huh?

I glance at him, and he's holding a blue flowered sundress of mine in his hands. I didn't pack the dress. I might be a city girl, but I know enough about the woods to know it's completely wrong for camping. The fabric is soft and billowy, and the spaghetti straps require a strapless bra. It's also extremely short and only goes to mid-thigh.

I squint my eyes at him. "You want me to wear that on a nature hike?"

"Yep." He tosses it at me and I catch it. "It's your next hotwife challenge."

Ohhh. Hey, I liked the first challenge. This one doesn't seem too difficult, though. It's not as bad as showering with the blinds open.

Well, except I didn't bring a bra to wear with the dress, but I suppose I can go braless. My breasts are large — especially for my tiny frame — but they're firm, so I don't always need to support them. I'm sure this will change as I get older, but I'm not there yet.

"Okay, sure. I'll wear it."

I pull the dress over my head and bend over, digging into my bag for clean underwear.

"No panties."

My head pops up and I look at Lucas. "What? No panties?"

Doesn't he see how short this dress is? A soft breeze might blow it up and I'll flash everyone looking in my direction.

"Yep, it's part of the challenge."

I shift uncomfortably.

Do I want to do this challenge? What are the chances we're going to see that many people on the trails? My pussy buzzes as I think about how I assumed I wouldn't see anyone in the shower, and yet I did. Ms. Kitty is a traitorous slut. She wants the entire campground to see my bare cooch. Okay, I kind of like the dirtiness of this challenge, but I don't want to sound too enthusiastic.

I give an exaggerated sigh. "Fine. No underwear."

As we step out of the tent, the breeze flutters the edge of my dress. I immediately feel naked. Oh shit, this might not be a good idea. I debate telling Lucas I changed my mind while he digs sandwiches out of the cooler for us. When we sit at the wooden picnic table, the dress barely covers my shaved pussy. Not good. I stand to tug the dress down as far as I can before sitting on it again.

Lucas smiles at me and takes a bite of his sandwich. I want to gripe about how dumb this idea is, but my hard nipples and a tingle from my core keep me quiet. I'm getting turned on, which I'm guessing is the point. Lucas better want more sexy times today. If this keeps up, I'm going to be all over him when we get back. Or maybe before.

We make small talk about the campsite and the weather while we eat. When we're finished with lunch, he takes my hand while we head towards the trail head. Thank God it's not a super breezy day. I have to keep my free hand near my thighs in case I need to rescue a sudden flyaway dress.

We pass a few couples in the campsite. Knowing the only thing stopping them from seeing me naked is the thin fabric sets Ms. Kitty buzzing. At the start of the trail, Lucas pauses and reads the sign about the two-mile walk. I'm keeping my eye out for people heading our way from down the trail, so I don't notice someone coming behind us until rocks and branches crunch under their feet.

A quick glance over my shoulder reveals a cute brown-haired guy that I'd guess is in his late 30s. He's alone, and wearing long pants and hiking boots, so I assume he's planning on walking the trail.

"Oh hey," he calls out and looks at Lucas.

Lucas turns and laughs. "Well, hi again!"

Uh, they know each other? Lucas must have interpreted my questioning glance.

"Jessica, this is Mike. I met him earlier when taking a shower. Mike, this is my gorgeous wife I was telling you about."

He was talking about me in the shower room? My pussy clenches and my inner thighs suddenly feel damp.

Mike laughs. "You weren't exaggerating. She *is* gorgeous."

Lust ripples through me, and my nipples pucker even more. I fight the urge to rub my thighs together. This is an odd introduction, but it's also erotic.

"Hi, Mike. It's nice to meet you."

I think I sound awkward as all fuck, but his eyes twinkle when he looks at me, so he must not notice.

"It's nice to meet you. Lucas was singing your praises this morning, but I like to put a face to the name."

When his eyes drop briefly to my chest, my body warms up. He definitely checked me out, but he's not being a perv about it. I enjoy being admired as long as the people do it respectfully. I'm not getting creepy vibes from Mike, so his peek turns me on even more.

He shifts his attention to the sign that Lucas is reading, and I study the two men together. They're both attractive, but I think Lucas is cuter. I married one sexy man.

Lucas turns to Mike. "Hey, want to walk with us?"

When Mike says, "Sure," Lucas winks at me. Uh-oh. What does my husband have planned? He only winks when he's up to something.

"Let's get going. We're burning daylight. Jessica, I want you to walk in front of us."

Um... yeah... It suddenly becomes clear what he's doing. He wants me to struggle to keep my dress down, knowing they're behind me. I will *not* give him the satisfaction of saying no.

"Sure," I purr at him and set off down the trail.

I don't even wait for them. If I'm in front, they have to go at my pace. The sound of their feet on the dirt path tells me they're behind me, and I slow my pace slightly and roll my hips as I walk to give them a sexy view of my ass.

Lucas and Mike chat about Oregon and various hiking trails as we walk. Every once in a while, a warm breeze blows over us and I have to rescue my dress. It's not too bad since the trees block the wind, but it really doesn't take much to make my dress flutter up.

"Jessica, pick some flowers to take back with us."

I was so busy thinking about them watching my ass, I didn't notice the pretty wildflowers along the trail. I glance back at the men and both are smiling at me.

Oh sure, Lucas wants me to struggle to bend over, but I'll show him. I crouch down instead of bending at the waist. My pussy lips slide apart in this position and I realize it's saving my modesty, but it feels even dirtier.

Fuck.

I quickly pick a couple of flowers and straighten up. I'm flushed and a throb from Ms. Kitty tells me she's getting impatient. Yeah, I know... we want Lucas's cock again.

We occasionally pass other people, but no one tries to talk to us other than a brief, "hello," or "have a good day." As we walk along, Lucas keeps telling me to pick flowers, and I keep crouching down to do it.

Each time I get more and more turned on. My lips are open slightly and I'm breathing heavily the longer the walk takes. By the time it loops back around, my brain is fuzzy and all I can think about is getting Lucas's cock inside me.

I see the sign that signals the end of the trail. I'm almost to freedom and Lucas's cock!

"Jessica, I want that flower over there."

Lucas gestures towards a flower, probably the last one I can pick before we leave the trail, and I'm suddenly brave.

Bending at the waist to pick this one, my dress rides up past my ass. If the men are looking at me, my shaved, wet pussy is on display. I take my time before standing, straightening my dress, and twitching my ass in their direction without looking at them.

I keep walking and I hear them talking, but it's low enough I can't make out what they are saying. They are following me and that's all that matters.

When we stop at the sign, Mike takes my hand and kisses the back of it. His voice is husky, and there is admiration in his gaze. I can tell he's turned on. "Thank you for a very interesting walk, Jessica. I'm glad I ran into you guys."

I smile sweetly at him. "Thanks for joining us."

He shares goodbyes with Lucas, and once he leaves, I turn to my husband. I'm vibrating with need.

"Lucas, I want…"

He puts his finger to my lips. "You just showed your bare pussy to a guy, and he liked what he saw."

Ms. Kitty clenches. "Really?"

"Yes." He runs his hand through my hair and caresses my cheekbone with his thumb. "He seemed interested in seeing more."

His words send a shiver down my spine. "How do you know?"

"He told me I could invite him on this type of nature walk whenever I wanted."

My heart skips a beat. "He did?"

He nods.

I lick my lips and eye my husband. While I enjoyed turning them both on, Lucas is the one I care about, and the one whose cock I need inside me right now.

I take his hand. "You have five minutes to get me back to the tent and get your cock in me before I explode."

He laughs. "Then we better hurry."

We're not exactly running back to our campsite, but we're speed walking fast enough that we catch a few eyes. I don't know what they think, and I don't care.

We tumble into the tent, and I barely get the zipper door closed before he's all over me. He doesn't bother removing any of his clothes. Since I'm not wearing panties, there's nothing in the way of him pulling his cock out and fucking me.

We're on top of the sleeping bag, and he ravishes my mouth as his cock slides inside me.

"God, yessss." I cry out and rock against him.

Wrapping my legs and arms around him, I meet him thrust for thrust. I'm still in my hiking boots, and I'm probably getting dirt everywhere, but I don't care.

We're like crazed animals as we claw at each other. He fucks me harder than he has in a long time. Each whack against Ms. Kitty shoots lightning through my core, and I'm moaning with each plunge.

When Lucas speeds up, I can tell he's about to come. As our gazes lock, we both peak. I cry out as waves of pleasure hit me, and he groans as he unloads ropes of sticky cum deep inside me. Watching him get lost in the pleasure intensifies my orgasm and it seems like the waves will never end.

When he slows down and stops, I slump down into the sleeping bag. "Oh God, you're going to kill me by the end of this trip."

He rolls to his side, pulls me close, and nuzzles my neck. When he speaks, his breath tickles me. "Maybe we shouldn't go on another hike. That was too strenuous."

"Mmm hmm." I'm floating in a fuzzy post-orgasmic haze. "Something more relaxing."

"Yeah," he agrees with me. "But tomorrow we're going swimming. We can't come here and not visit the beautiful lake."

I squint up at him. He's got a devious glint in his eye. Uh-oh. What does he have planned for me at the lake?

Chapter 3

I swear it's the crack of dawn when Lucas wakes me. He shoves a granola bar and a banana at me.

"Baby, eat some breakfast. I want to hit the lake early, before it gets crowded."

Struggling to sit up, I fumble with the wrapper on the bar. I blink at him, confused. "Wait, what time is it?"

My brain is not ready to wake up.

He shrugs. "Does it matter? The sun is up."

Hmm, is it? The window isn't open, but the campgrounds are quiet and it's not that bright in the tent.

Camping sort of sucks. If I wasn't getting so much sex, I'd say I was never going camping again, but I'm having fun since he's keeping me needy and at a low simmer all the time. He could persuade me to do this occasionally if it includes a weekend of sexual abandon.

Yawning, I finish my granola bar and banana before I get dressed. It's going to be a warm day, so I put on my tiny, ass-hugging shorts and a white tank top. I debate on a bra, but opt to skip it. Maybe it's his turn to be distracted. I'll use the power of my tits to mesmerize him. We're not hiking, so my sandals are good enough for a walk around the campgrounds.

We separate for a few minutes to finish our morning routine. When we reunite, my teeth are minty fresh and my long, blonde hair is in a braid. I'll shower later after our walk, and the braid will keep my hair from being too crazy if it gets windy. I'm ready to face the day. Or at least as ready as I'll be.

Lucas has a beach bag slung over his shoulder and I eye it as I approach him. "What's in the bag?"

"Nothing you need to worry about."

He kisses me. I stand on my tippy toes so I can wrap my arms around his neck and plaster my body to his. I know he's only kissing to distract me, but I welcome it anyway. A soft tingle runs through me. Uh-oh, Ms. Kitty is waking up.

Lucas breaks off the kiss. I hold on to his neck and try to tempt him into more. I purr, "We don't need to visit the lake, do we? We could go back to bed and have more fun."

He chuckles and shakes his head. "Nope, we're going to the lake. I didn't come all this way to not see it."

I want to tell him a two-hour drive isn't far, but I hold my tongue. Fine, back to Plan A: torturing him with my bouncing boobies all day. That might be more fun, anyway.

We walk past several tents and barely anyone is awake. It's a short walk down a dirt path to the lake, and when we get there, it's deserted and peaceful. It's one of the major attractions at the campground for families. I've heard it's busy mid-day when everyone is swimming.

There's a dock that runs out to the deeper part of the lake for people to jump off. No way in hell is that happening this morning. We walk past the dock, and Lucas drops the beach bag at the edge of the dry sand.

I'm only planning to wade into the water, so I kick off my sandals and dip my toes in. Okay, yeah, that's a little too cool for me. I'd need a hot day before I'd go swimming — preferably in a pool at a hotel.

When Lucas walks into the shallows, I follow him. The water laps softly against my ankles as I splash around playfully, avoiding any slippery rocks. My writer's mind expects a sea monster to grab my legs and pull me under to trap me in the seaweed. Luckily, the water is clear, so I can tell nothing is swimming at me. After a few moments, I relax and enjoy the serenity.

Lucas closes his eyes and breathes deeply before opening them and smiling at me. "Let's stay here awhile. I love being by the water."

"Me too." The tranquility of the morning settles over me. I lean against him and sigh. This isn't bad at all.

He wraps his arms around me and gives me a quick smooch. "I'm glad you're having fun."

"Mm hmm." I melt against him, enjoying his strength and warmth. No need to tell him I'm only having fun because of all the sex.

He kisses me again, but this time he takes his time with it. A glow of desire builds, and I press closer against him. Our tongues twine together as each stroke shoots electricity through me.

Mmm, now this is more like it. He slides his hands under my tank top, and I tremble when he skims the sensitive skin on my side. He knows how to drive me wild.

As he continues to explore with his hands, I moan when he caresses the soft skin next to my breasts. My nipples harden and I ache for him to play with them. But we're in public and someone could walk past any moment. Shit, we really should behave, but what's the fun in that?

When he pulls back, I mewl in protest. Dammit, it was getting good.

"Baby, it's time for your next hotwife challenge."

All my nerve endings tingle. "Oooh, yes?"

What could he have planned here? Ms. Kitty is fully awake and the slickness between my legs has me scanning the wooded area next to us. Whatever he's got planned for me is bound to turn me on even more. I bet I could find a secluded spot and ravish him. We don't need to go back to the tent to fuck.

His eyes twinkle when he grins. "I want you to go for a swim."

That gets my attention, and I bark out a laugh. "Oh, hell no. The water is cold, and I didn't bring a bathing suit."

He studies me for a second, and his voice is firm. "You're going skinny dipping."

My mouth opens slightly. I'm about to protest when he slides his hands back under my shirt again and cups my breasts. When he tugs on my nipples, I gasp and bite my lip to keep from crying out. Fiery sparks rush through me from his touch. I'm already wet, so he's adding fuel to the fire.

His voice turns silky smooth. "Come on baby, this will be fun."

Ugh, it's impossible to think when he's tweaking my nipples. His hands feel so damn good. If he kept doing this all day, I'd agree to anything.

I finally give in and nod my head. I'll take a quick dip and call it good. No one is here yet. It'll be fine.

We get out of the water and I take a quick glance around to verify we really are alone. I pull off my tank top and drop my shorts and panties.

Fuck, this is so wrong, but as soon as I'm naked, an illicit thrill makes me feel alive. This is naughty and I sort of love it.

I drop my clothes on top of the beach bag, and Lucas follows me back to the water. Wait, what is he doing? Oh shit, I didn't even notice his shorts were his swim shorts. He pulls his shirt off, tosses it back towards our stuff, and enters the water with me.

Fuuuuck, this is way too cold. "How long do I have to stay in the water?"

"Until I've decided you've won the challenge."

I'm *so* going to pay him back for this someday. I wade in further and suck in a breath as the water rises to my waist.

Someone calls from the shore. "Hey guys!"

Oh fuck, it's Mike! I dip into the water up to my neck and hold in several swear words as the coldness envelopes me.

Lucas laughs, and he sounds delighted. "Hey Mike, do you want to join us?"

Hmm... what are the chances Mike shows up at the lake while I'm skinny dipping? This is suspicious.

"Nah," Mike calls out. "I'll watch from the shore. It's too cold for a swim."

Yeah, no shit. I shiver, but it's from more than the water temperature. Mike saying he's going to watch gives an added zing to this experience. It also proves that anyone could walk down here at any moment and catch us.

Lucas grins at him. "I guess we'll have to give you something to watch."

I don't know what my dear husband has planned, but he's going to have to get fully wet to do it. I take off and swim further into the lake towards the dock. Lucas follows me and when I reach the end of the dock, I hold on to the edge as Lucas catches up.

He swims up behind me and presses my breasts against the wood. The contact with the rough panels almost makes me moan, but knowing my luck, any sound I make would echo over the water.

Mike walks towards the dock and stands on the shore, observing us. Hell, he really does plan on watching.

Lucas's hand slides between my legs, and he rubs my pussy. "I could fuck you right here, and you'd let me, wouldn't you?"

As his finger slides against my clit, I can't hold back my moan. "Yessss."

He whispers in my ear. "I want to fuck you. Ask me to fuck you while he's watching."

Does Lucas have an exhibitionist streak in him? Fuck, this is hot. I moan and pant. "Please fuck me."

I should tell him to stop. We shouldn't be doing this in public — and definitely not while Mike is here — but I can't help myself. I want Lucas's cock, right here, right now.

He thrusts a finger inside me, and I grind on it while I beg. "Please, Lucas? Please fuck me. I need you."

He's nimble and his fingers move fast inside me. We're both breathing heavily and my head is spinning. "Oh god, I can't think. Fuck me, please."

He kisses the side of my neck, and I stop caring that Mike is watching. I need my husband's cock inside me and I'll do anything to get it. I widen my legs and grip the wood firmly, daring him to fill me.

He continues to finger fuck me, and I go wild from the pleasure. Arching my back, I push against him to force his fingers in deeper. I keep my eyes glued on Mike, and he's staring at us with a smile on his face. I'm not sure he knows what we're doing. I'm guessing he can tell Lucas is up to something since Lucas's mouth is still on my neck. Each tiny bite and lick makes me coo in delight.

Lucas pulls his fingers free and moves his hips forward until the tip of his cock presses against my wetness. My mind is a buzzing mess of static. He pauses there to tease my pussy, and I'm dying to feel him inside me. He gives a low growl in his throat as he gently thrusts against me, but doesn't enter me. Holy fuck, he's going to make me insane with lust.

He's barely poking his hardness against me, and I throw my head back and moan loudly. Oh god, this feels incredible, but I need him to fuck me.

Lucas pulls back. "I want you to beg."

Oh god, what more does he want? I can feel my pussy clenching and I whimper. "Please fuck me. I need your cock."

He stops moving, leaving his cock nestled between my folds, but still not inside me. I try to rotate my hips to create friction.

"Baby, you keep doing that and I'm going to come without fucking you. Do you want that?"

My brain fizzles at his words. Shit, no, no, no. I stop all movement.

He continues. "Say you're a dirty slut who loves knowing someone is watching us."

A wave of shame hits me, but he's right. I'm loving this. My pussy throbs from the forbidden pleasure as I blurt out, "Yes, I'm a filthy slut who's getting turned on by Mike watching. Now please fuck me... Please!"

Lucas chuckles and releases me. "You won the challenge. Now we can leave."

Whaaaat? I'm dizzy and confused, my entire body throbbing in protest. "You're not going to fuck me?"

"Not yet. That's later."

He swims towards the shore.

I stare after him for a few heartbeats before following. Mike walks over to the edge of the water to greet Lucas as he gets out. Lucas's shorts are wet and clinging to his body, exposing his visible hardness underneath them. I can't believe he didn't slip his cock inside me. This game of his is torture for both of us.

Shit. Now I'm stuck in the water since I'm naked. Damn those two. I'm in the shallow area and I stay submerged past my breasts. Without Lucas fingering me and distracting me, I'm reminded of how cold the water is. Once we get back to the tent, I'm going to bundle up in my sleeping bag and Lucas will have to rub me all over to warm me up. I'll convince him that Ms. Kitty is freezing and needs lots of attention.

Lucas calls to me from the shore. "I'm adding to the challenge. Get out of the water while we watch."

I almost protest, but worry that Lucas will change the rules yet again. Oh god, do I want to do this? My stomach muscles tighten as my heart rate speeds up. I close my eyes for a moment and imagine rising like a goddess with the water streaming off me.

Okay, I can do this.

When I open my eyes, Lucas is holding a towel for me. Well, I guess I know what was in the beach bag. This proves he planned this all along.

As if I didn't know.

I draw in a long breath and stand up straight. The slight breeze against my wet skin creates goosebumps, and my nipples harden into sharp peaks. The hot and heavy gaze of both men gives me a shiver of pleasure as I straighten my shoulders and slink towards them.

Wet heat flares between my legs, as I keep my eyes locked on to Lucas. Even though I'm not looking at Mike, I can feel the lust pouring from him the closer I get.

I'll show them. I ignore the open towel and put my back to the guys as I bend over to get my clothes. They've seen this view before, so now they get another peek.

Turning to face them, I shimmy my panties and shorts up my wet legs. It's a bit of a struggle, so my breasts sway as I work to get the shorts buttoned. When I drag my tank top over my head, it sticks to my skin. Since it's white, the pink of my nipples shows through the fabric.

Both guys are silent, spellbound, and my bravery has me practically vibrating with need.

I slide my sandy feet into my sandals and toss my head defiantly. "I need a shower. Lucas, you coming?"

I don't wait for him and head off, twitching my ass in their direction. I hear Lucas say a quick goodbye to Mike as he runs to catch up with me.

"Bye Mike, see you at eight!"

What's happening at eight? Pleasurable anticipation hits my core and I'm so distracted, I almost trip. I right myself just in time and look over my shoulder at Lucas as he slows down to walk with me.

"We're seeing Mike tonight?"

He gives me a slow grin. "Yes. Another challenge."

My mind glazes over as I try to imagine what that could be. Mike has already seen me fully naked.

How far is this going to go?

Chapter 4

The walk to our tent is quiet and I savor the feeling of being alone with Lucas. I can barely contain my excitement. As soon as we duck inside the tent, I turn to face him. His eyes are hooded and dark, and his lips form a half-smile.

He sits down, cross-legged, on our sleeping bags and pulls me into his lap. I fit my ass against his hardness and wiggle, pretending I need to get comfortable. I'm going to take a shower soon, but he deserves a little teasing first for what he did to me at the lake.

His hand travels slowly down my arm until he cups a breast. I gasp softly as my nipples tighten and my pussy pulses with pleasure.

His fingers squeeze my tit, and he kisses my neck, murmuring against my skin. "I was so close to fucking you in the lake."

My breath hitches in response, and Lucas slides his hand from my breast, down my flat belly, dipping beneath the waistband of my shorts. His palm is warm against my bare skin, and I drop my head back as pleasure ripples through me.

So much for me teasing him. He's doing a good job of working me up more than I already was. I want to know what's happening tonight before desire fogs my brain and I forget to ask. "Why is Mike coming to visit?"

Lucas unbuttons my shorts so he can reach more skin. He's intent on what he's doing, but he kisses my nose before he answers. "I invited him for s'mores."

Uh-huh, right. There's no way I believe he's coming for s'mores. "That's all? Nothing else?"

He chuckles and slides his hand further down my shorts, brushing his fingers over my wet panties and rubbing me through the fabric.

"Ohhh god," I moan.

I'm so distracted, I don't notice he didn't answer. Ms. Kitty is buzzing, and I'm desperate for him to fuck me. I need him.

"Are you ready to beg for my cock again?" His voice is husky and his fingers slide my panties aside so he can rub my clit.

I nod and then shake my head no. I'm so aroused, I can't think straight. What did he ask? Oh yeah, I need to beg for his cock.

My voice is barely above a whisper. "God, Lucas. Please fuck me."

He chuckles softly. "No, that's for later."

Whaaat? He told me to beg, and now he's not going to fuck me? I want to argue with him, but I'm too turned on to think straight. Fuck, he's driving me crazy.

I cup my hands around his face and pull him down for a kiss. Our tongues duel for dominance as I ride his fingers.

As soon as our mouths part, I ask, "Did you tell Mike about the challenge?"

"Yes." He kisses me again, and I try to take control of the kiss, but he keeps pulling away.

I whine in frustration. "Why aren't you fucking me?"

He lifts his head and smiles at me. "Because you have to wait for tonight."

Oh, hell no. He's teased me long enough that I don't want to wait. I can get his cock now, and I'll still want it again later. I grip his hair and kiss him passionately.

He groans and pulls away, laughing. "You're so impatient."

I lean up and nip at his bottom lip. "I love your cock, and I'm always hungry for it."

He tries to change the topic. "Well, we're going to shower — " I look up at him, hopeful, and he cuts himself off. "No, get that look off your face. We're showering alone."

Dammit.

He continues. "Then I need to go buy some more firewood. You're going to stay here and think about what I might ask you to do tonight for the challenge."

He slides his hand out of my shorts. Yeah, this isn't going how I hoped.

"Fine," I huff at him and climb off his lap. His laugh is infectious, and it coaxes a smile from me. As much as I claim to dislike being edged, a part of me also loves it.

I knew Lucas had plans for this weekend, but this seems beyond having a vague idea of what he wants to do. It really seems like everything he's doing is calculated, and it's leading me towards, I don't know?

Fucking Mike?

Shit, do I want it? As I carry my shower supplies with me to the bathroom, a wave of lust rolls through me, and Ms. Kitty flutters in response. Yeah, who am I kidding? I want to fuck Mike. I don't want to assume this is where the weekend is leading, because I told Lucas I wanted to go slow with the hotwife plans. But a weekend of escalating challenges is slow enough, and I'm ready to take the next step.

This camping trip is exactly why I love Lucas so much. How many husbands plan an entire weekend set around thrilling their wife with little adventures aimed towards turning her into a crazed nympho?

I'm so fucking lucky.

Lucas takes longer than necessary to buy wood at the tiny store on the campgrounds. I suspect he's off planning something for tonight.

I'm showered, dressed, and sitting at the picnic table, lost in a daydream of Mike fucking me while Lucas watches. When I hear voices getting closer, I lift my head and squint into the bright sunlight.

A man and woman are walking past our campsite. I recognize them from the day before. It's the guy who smiled at me while I was showering with the blinds open.

He winks at me. I suck in my breath from shock and feel myself blush. A second later, my nipples harden and I shift my position so I can press my pussy against the wooden bench.

The woman gives me a tiny wave and a knowing smile as they continue past, but neither of them greet me. Ohhhh fuck, did he tell her he saw me in the shower? If so, she seems to approve. I hope she got a nice hard pounding after she found out.

My daydream switches to thinking about those two going at it in their tent before I shake my head to clear it. Fuck, Lucas needs to get back. I'm getting turned on by every little thing.

When Lucas walks back from the store carrying a bundle of wood, I hop up from the bench and rush to him. "Where have you been?"

My voice is deeper than normal. I know I sound turned on and excited. I'm sure he can tell as well.

He gives me a speculative look. "I had other business to attend to. Something fun for tonight."

Tonight. I've gotta wait for tonight.

He sets the wood down by the campfire and walks back to me. I try one last time to seduce him into the sleeping bag. I walk my fingers up his arm and rub his neck. Using my most seductive tone, I purr at him, "So now we go make sweet, sweet love for hours, right?"

When I run my other hand over his chest, he stops me by wrapping his arms around me and holding me tight. "Baby, you have to wait. We have a hot date tonight."

I raise my eyebrows at him. He's finally admitting this is more than a meetup with Mike for s'mores? "Who said this was a date tonight? I thought we were going to stuff ourselves sick with marshmallows and chocolate."

He laughs and his eyes sparkle. "Trust me."

"Hmmm, maybe," I tease.

He kisses me, and I melt against him. After a few moments, his hands move to my hips and he pulls me to him. His cock is hard, and he rubs against me as he asks, "What do you think is going to happen tonight?"

My imagination is running wild, and I'm giddy with anticipation. "I think we're going to play a game."

"A game?"

I tip my head up and give him a slow grin. "Yeah, a sexy game."

"What kind of game would that be?"

"A hot one." I can be mysterious as much as he can.

He grins and kisses my nose. "You're such a bad girl."

"Yep." I laugh and push him away from me. "That's why you love me."

If he won't fuck me right now, I need to find something to occupy my mind. Otherwise, I'm sure to work myself into a frenzy. I blow him a kiss and climb into the tent to grab my e-reader. I'll read a clean romance and hopefully cool down a bit.

Nope. My clean romance didn't get my mind off tonight, and I tried to guess what Lucas is going to suggest. I finally settled on strip poker. I'm not sure how he expects us to do it while the people at the campgrounds are still awake, but I think Lucas is going to get me naked somehow.

When I go outside, I lounge in one of the camping chairs we brought with us. Lucas keeps himself occupied by sharpening the end of three sticks into points. Oh fuck, maybe we really are having s'mores.

The rest of the day drags. By the time Mike's supposed to arrive, my panties are wet and I'm jumping at every footstep I hear. Mike is five minutes late — not like I was watching the clock on my phone or anything. When he finally arrives, the sun is setting and Lucas has the campfire blazing.

The guys greet each other like they are the best of pals, confirming my suspicion they were making plans on the sly. Whatever. They can have their secrets. I'm sure I'll find out soon enough.

Lucas breaks me out of my sexy daydream. "Jessica, baby?"

"Yes, love?"

"Can you get the chocolate bars from the cooler?"

"Sure." I stand up to head past him towards the cooler. He grabs my wrist and pulls me close to him.

"You're so beautiful," he murmurs in my ear and then tilts my chin up so he can kiss me. "After you get the chocolate, I want you to put on the sundress you wore on the hike yesterday. Don't wear any panties."

My heart skips a beat at the thought of having so little clothes on again. Oh yeah, this is totally going to be strip poker. He's making sure I end up naked. I nod my agreement, unable to speak, as he kisses me again. When he walks away from me, I hurry to the cooler. I practically toss the chocolates on the picnic table and hightail it into the tent to change.

I strip quickly and slip the sundress over my head. I breathe a sigh of relief when I don't feel uncomfortable wearing the dress with nothing underneath. Hell, it almost feels normal.

When I get back to the guys, Lucas has arranged our camping chairs in a half circle around the campfire, and facing away from the main campground. I still don't see any pack of cards out. Huh. What is he up to?

Lucas gestures towards the middle chair. "Sit down, my goddess."

I give him a soft smile. Okay, I don't mind this so far. After all, I am his goddess, right?

Mike sits in the chair on my left. His eyes are dark with desire as he greets me. "Nice to see you again, Jessica."

I echo his sentiment and peek at him as I settle in, making sure I sit on my dress since I'm not wearing panties. Whenever I saw him before, I was always buzzing and mentally fuzzy from lust, so this is the first time I'm able to study him. He's wearing cargo shorts, a short-sleeved t-shirt, and sandals. His legs are muscular and toned, like he hikes regularly. He's not a huge guy, but he's got a sleek and powerful build. I can tell he either works out often or has a job with considerable manual labor.

When Lucas passes out the s'mores supplies, Mike's fingers catch my attention and fascinate me. His fingers are long, slender, and almost delicate. I could easily imagine him playing an instrument with them, or rubbing my clit...

Shit. Focus, Jessica.

"So..." I look expectantly at Lucas. "What are we doing?"

His mouth twists, and his eyes shine in the firelight. "Time for the challenge."

Even though I was expecting this, I still get a thrill and my pussy grows even more wet. I set the s'mores supplies on the side table attached to the camping chair and ask, "What do I have to do?"

I'm hoping I don't sound too eager. Heck, I might say no to whatever it is just to mess with him. Fair's fair, right?

He leans forward with an intense expression on his face. "I want you to spread your legs and rub your clit."

Uh... what? "Right here, right now? People might see."

"Yes?" He sweeps his arms in the direction of the campground behind me. "Who is going to see you?"

I realize he put me in this chair on purpose. Damn, he's devious. I glance over my shoulder. Nobody's close by, and it's getting darker and harder to see very far. Someone would have to be close to know what was going on.

I close my eyes and take several deep breaths. This is crazy, but I'm going to do it. I guess Mike is going to get another glimpse of Ms. Kitty.

I pull the front of my dress to my waist and spread my knees, revealing my smooth mound. The air is warm and dry, and the part of my sundress I'm sitting on is getting damp. I drop my hand between my legs and slide my fingers between my folds.

"Open your eyes," Lucas orders.

I obey and open my eyes wide as I continue to stroke myself.

Mike's eyes are glued to me — or more specifically, my pussy. Fuck, that's hot. Knowing both guys are watching me be a filthy slut quickly spirals me towards an orgasm. My thighs tremble as I rub myself faster and faster. I can feel my juices flowing down my inner thigh.

I glance at Lucas to make sure he's okay with this. He's watching my fingers intently.

"Can I come?" I ask him.

"No," he answers immediately. "Not yet."

I whimper loudly. "Please, let me come?"

Lucas's voice is gruff. "No. Keep rubbing. You can't come."

I try to stifle my moans as I plunge two fingers inside me and rock my hips up to meet them. What does Mike think about all of this? I steal a glance at him.

Mike's cock is visible, hard underneath his shorts. Mmm, yummy. I wish he'd pull his cock out so I could see it. I wet my lips while I think about sucking him in front of Lucas. Yeah, I'm such a dirty girl.

"I think she's close," Mike says in a husky voice.

"God, I am! Please, can I come?" I beg.

"No," Lucas replies firmly. "Keep rubbing."

He's sounding like a broken record. I cry out softly and move my fingers from my pussy to circle around my sensitive clit. I'm beyond being able to stay quiet, and little peeps and moans slip out. The pleasure builds, threatening to overwhelm me.

"Fuuuck." I moan loud enough for Lucas to hear me. I'm almost beyond caring whether he'll give me permission. I want Mike to see me come. Fuck, at this point I'd let a whole football team watch me orgasm. I just need it. Now.

"Jessica." Lucas's sharp voice breaks through my lust. "Stop touching."

Noooo. I don't want to stop. He was supposed to tell me to keep going. I lock gazes with Lucas and continue rubbing myself. My thigh muscles quiver and I'm going to explode any second.

Lucas's voice holds a harsh warning this time. "Jessica, stop or you won't like the consequences."

Ugh. I debate it for one second, then pull my hand from between my legs. Shit... fuck... my brain is a pile of mush.

Lucas stands up and holds his hand out to me. "Come here, baby."

I stand up shakily, uncertain what is going on. I can't think of anything but getting a cock inside me — either guy's cock would do.

Lucas leads me behind the tent and out of sight from Mike. He pulls me into his arms and gives me a toe-curlingly deep kiss. I lose myself in him as our tongues twirl together. When he breaks off the kiss, I mewl in protest. God, he's being so mean.

"Jessica, baby, do you want to fuck Mike tonight? I'd like it, but the choice is yours."

My entire body buzzes. He just handed me the golden ticket, and I wasn't expecting it. I assumed he was going to edge me once we got started.

Lucas's eyes bore into mine and a flush runs from my toes to my head. My nipples harden and wetness trickles down my inner thigh. He's waiting for my answer.

I link my fingers with his and give them a soft squeeze. "Yes, my love. I want to fuck Mike."

He lets out a deep breath like he was nervous about my answer, and then grins at me. "Then let's do this."

My pulse quickens as desire coils in my stomach. It's time for me to really become a hotwife.

I'm ready.

Chapter 5

The night air is cool. I shiver and Lucas pulls me closer. I snuggle in, and he rubs his thumb along my cheek.

"Baby, you can change your mind, even in the middle. Say the word and I'll stop it. Okay?"

I nod, and a rush of love for him zips through me. I'm glad we're doing this together.

He doesn't move right away, and I glance at him curiously. "What's wrong?"

"Oh, I just…" He looks hesitant. "I was thinking I'd stay outside the tent while you fuck him."

Huh. "You don't want to watch?"

He shakes his head. "Not tonight, baby. I want to listen and imagine what you're doing."

In my fantasy, he was always watching. As long as he's close by, I can adjust. I rub my cheek against his chest. Lucas smells like soap — a little musky and a little spicy — and it soothes me. "Okay, my love."

Lucas kisses me again, coaxing my lips open and swirling his tongue with mine. I get lost in the moment and my brain is fuzzy when he breaks the kiss off.

His eyes blaze with intensity. "Wait in the tent for Mike."

Nodding slowly, I enter the tent and kneel on my sleeping bag, my ass resting on my feet. I'm already wet from almost coming, and my entire body buzzes with anticipation. My breathing shallows, and I can feel the heat radiating off me. I'm turned on and practically dripping with excitement. All the minor challenges leading up to this moment did exactly what they should do — I'm needy and desperate to bang someone other than my husband.

Now that I've agreed to fuck Mike, I'm not sure what the protocol is. Do I take off my dress? Do I keep it on? What will another cock feel like? It's been years since I've fucked anyone but Lucas. A million thoughts run through my mind and my heart rate spikes at the thought of being totally naked in front of someone other than Lucas.

A few moments later, Mike appears at the tent entrance alone and Lucas calls out, "Jessica, I'm going to be right outside."

I can see his silhouette through the tent wall as he moves a chair outside the door flap. I feel safer knowing he's right there.

"Okay, love." I turn my attention to Mike and the crazy, slutty thing I'm about to do.

Mike gives me a sexy grin as he ducks into the tent. His eyes roam my body hungrily, taking in every inch of me. Ms. Kitty pulses in response and the ache between my legs grows more insistent.

Mike is too tall to stand up, so he drops on his knees in front of me. His gaze is possessive, as if he knows I'm his to play with. I can feel heat rising in my cheeks in response.

Mike clears his throat before speaking, and his voice is husky. "You want to do this?"

I nod, unable to find any words as excitement and nerves churn inside me. Oh, yeah, there is no doubt about it. If he doesn't get his cock inside me soon, I'm going to beg.

He moves closer to me and brushes the hair out of my face before kissing me passionately. Mmm, now this is more like it. I kiss him back with abandon as I run my hands underneath his shirt. He's more muscular than Lucas and I explore wherever my hands can reach from his belt line to his shoulders. His chest has a light covering of hair and I'm curious what my nipples brushing against him would feel like. Will it feel different from Lucas?

Right when I expect him to deepen the kiss and really go for it, he pulls back. "Lucas agreed to let you be my slut tonight. I want to see my slut naked."

My skin prickles with desire and I fight the urge to say 'Yes, sir,' as I pull the dress over my head. I drop it to the floor next to me and push my chest out, drawing attention to my breasts. Thanks to my dear husband, I'm naked since the dress was the only thing I had on.

Mike lets out a low whistle as his eyes scan every inch of me, lingering for a few seconds on my breasts. My nipples harden, and I want him to touch me everywhere.

Mike takes my hand and tugs, so I rise on my knees. Ms. Kitty does a happy dance as he presses against me and I feel his thick hardness through his shorts. His cock is what I'm here for. Is he bigger than Lucas? Will he reach places inside me that Lucas's cock doesn't? The unknown of fucking someone new is thrilling, and I'm extra sensitive to every brush against my skin.

He bends so his lips are millimeters away from mine. My heart races as he kisses me deeply, sliding his tongue into my mouth, exploring every inch. He tastes like cinnamon and smells like smokiness and spice. Everything about him is new, and all my senses are alive. He runs his hands down to cup my ass and pulls me closer against him.

Electricity sparks between us. I moan when he breaks off the kiss and nibbles his way down my neck. "You're so damn sexy, Jessica."

His words send shivers down my spine, and wetness coats my inner thighs as he pushes me onto my back. I don't hold in my sighs of pleasure as his hands explore my body. Every time he hits a ticklish spot, I gasp. Lucas is close enough to hear every sound, and I really hope he's enjoying this as much as I am.

As Mike moves down to kiss my stomach, he murmurs, "I can't wait to fuck you," against the sensitive skin at my navel, and my head spins. Somehow I always imagined my first time with another guy would be rough and wild, but so far Mike is doing everything he can to work me into a frenzy.

He continues lower, placing featherlight kisses all along the path until he reaches my shaved pussy.

"Spread your legs for me," he demands softly, and I open my legs so he can move between them.

I really wasn't expecting him to go down on me, but I'm so turned on, he could do whatever he wanted and I wouldn't care. He spreads my nether lips open with his hands, and his tongue is magical. I arch into him and clutch his shoulders as waves of pleasure course through me.

I'm not being quiet, and each swirl of his tongue makes me cry out in ecstasy. Fuck, this is amazing. I was dumb for hesitating when Lucas suggested I fuck other guys.

He slides two fingers inside me and starts fingerfucking me slowly. I grip the sleeping bag beneath me as I spiral towards my orgasm. He removes his hand and pushes my legs open wider as he plunges his tongue into my pussy.

"Fuuuck," I cry out, bucking my hips towards his mouth. When he speeds up his sucking and licking, the pleasure is too much for me to handle. I scream out as my climax crashes into me. Spikes of electricity ripple from my fingers to my toes as he continues to lick me.

When I come down from my high, Mike smiles up at me with a satisfied expression. He kisses his way back up my body, and I shiver as the cool air hits the wetness left by his lips.

He removes his shirt and shorts before covering my body and kissing me deeply. Our tongues swirl together as I taste myself on him. I moan against his mouth and try to grind against him. Even though I just came, I still want his cock.

Knowing that Lucas is listening makes this experience amazing. God, I hope he's stroking to this. Thinking about him being turned on by what a slut I am turns me on even more. I wouldn't want to do any of this without him.

Mike pulls away from me, and I mewl in protest until I realize he's repositioning himself. He teases my entrance for a moment with the head of his cock and I swear he's playing 'Just The Tip' with my pussy. Each short thrust makes me needier. I try to time my movements with his to force him inside me, but can't. This is making me crazier. I need it all.

With one powerful push, he sinks into me as I buck against him and cry out, "Ohhh, god."

His cock is thicker than I expect, and he stretches me as he burrows deep. I gasp at the sensation of him filling me up, inch by inch. He's gentle yet forceful, each thrust stronger than the last, until I'm almost clawing at him, desperate.

"Oh god, fuck me harder. Please?"

My words spur him on and he whacks against my pussy vigorously. Holy fuck. I wrap my legs around him and cling to his neck as the pleasure almost overwhelms me.

"Do you like my cock?" He's panting as he thrusts into me, and I can only chant, "Yes, yes, yes," as he drives me wild and fucks me with abandon.

My heart pounds in my chest, and the pleasure builds in layers as I'm reeling towards ecstasy. Mike picks up the pace, slamming his hips against mine.

Lucas fucks me hard sometimes, but it doesn't feel the same with Mike. Everything Lucas does has love behind it, but Mike and I have the mutual goal of only seeking pleasure. It makes fucking Mike dirtier and I want to be the sluttiest version of myself with him.

Stars pop on the edge of my vision as I rock against him, meeting him thrust for thrust. Tension coils low in my belly as I strain against him. After all the edging and teasing today, I need something more or I won't come.

Moving my hands to my breasts, I massage them and roll my nipples between my fingers as he hammers into me. My squeals of delight turn into long moans the closer I get.

He growls and fucks me harder. I'm so desperate, I move one hand to my pussy. Oh, god, I need to come. I rub my clit in fast circles until I can't take it anymore.

I throw my head back and scream as my second orgasm rips through me. My body convulses and my thighs quiver. He's like a machine, fucking me hard and fast through my orgasm. I'm panting and can't catch my breath.

He pulls my legs up, grips me under my knees and jackhammers into me from a new angle. Oh, holy fuck. Every nerve ending is on fire, and my brain switches off while he pummels into me relentlessly. I hear moans and words coming out of my mouth, but I don't know what I'm saying. Nothing matters other than the pleasure.

He tenses right before he comes and groans as he explodes. His cock pulses as he coats my cave walls with ropes of sticky cum. He slows down his thrusts as he fucks it back up into me, and time loses all meaning.

My brain is mush when he finally collapses beside me on the sleeping bag. We lay there for a few moments in silence, letting our breathing slow down until we can move again.

"Wow," I whisper when my brain works again.

He gives a soft laugh. "Wow is right."

I lie there blissfully, dazed and in ecstasy, while Mike caresses my fingers and absentmindedly twists my wedding ring. He appears to be just as wooly headed as I am.

I glance down at our intertwined fingers, focusing my gaze on my wedding ring. How is Lucas doing? Is he wondering what is going on right now? Is he aching for me?

Ms. Kitty gives a soft hum, and I almost smile. Yes, Lucas is the missing piece. I'm relaxed and tired from fucking Mike, but I'm longing for Lucas's embrace. He needs to hold me and let me know nothing has changed. I have to be sure that he enjoyed this, and I want him to fuck me with all the pent-up desire he's been holding in while he listened through the wall.

Mike stirs and brings my hand up to his mouth to kiss the back of it. "Thank you for a lovely evening, Jessica."

I grin at him. "You're welcome."

Lucas and I are leaving tomorrow, and I'm sure we'll never cross paths with Mike again, which is perfectly fine. I'm grateful for everything Mike did this weekend to help make my first hotwife experience enjoyable. I'll never forget him and I'm betting he'll think back on this weekend from time to time. Hopefully, he'll stroke while doing so.

I watch Mike get dressed. When he's finished, we both smile and exchange soft goodbyes as he leaves the tent. He and Lucas talk for a moment, and I hear my wonderful husband thanking Mike for giving me a pleasurable evening. Yeah, Lucas is a good guy.

When Lucas enters the tent, his eyes are glazed with lust and yearning. He quickly zips up the door flap and yanks his clothes off. His cock juts straight out and I swear I can see it pulsate. I lick my lips with anticipation as he drops to the ground and crawls towards me.

Every movement he makes tells me I'm about to get fucked hard, and I welcome it.

Chapter 6

"Spread your legs," Lucas demands hoarsely.

I don't hesitate and part my legs, assuming he's going to crawl between them and fuck me. When he stops to turn a lantern on, it gives me pause. Oh shit, what is he doing?

The campfire is down to glowing embers. Inside the tent it's shadowy, and details aren't crisp. Him turning the light on puts me on full display. Wetness slides down the crack of my ass and an illicit delight rushes through me. This is some other guy's cum leaking out of me.

Lucas continues to crawl towards me and pauses with his face right above my pussy, and he examines a soaked Ms. Kitty. I lean up on my elbows to watch him. I'm still not sure what he is doing.

When he runs his fingers up and down my slit, gathering the wetness and rubbing my clit in circles, my toes curl from the pleasure. I rock my hips against his hand, but his eyes never leave my pussy, like he's fascinated at how messy I am.

He pushes two fingers inside me slowly, and I moan, "Oh god, yes."

As soon as his fingers are in as far as they can go, he starts finger fucking me roughly. The bliss is intense and I arch my back to meet his thrusts. It's difficult to keep my eyes open, but I need to see his enjoyment. Tonight wasn't only about my pleasure. If we ever do this again, I have to know he wants it as much as I do.

He abruptly stops the movement of his hand and pulls his fingers out, examining how they glisten. Dang, my husband really is a bit of a perv if he's so fascinated by another guy's cum. When he gives one of his fingers a small lick, a flush ripples over me and my eyes widen.

His tongue darts out of his mouth, as if he's savoring the flavor, and then he grins at me. "Tastes like you."

Oh god, he's such a goof. I sit up and reach for him. "Lucas, if you don't get your cock inside — "

He doesn't let me finish as he launches himself at me and pushes me onto my back. He silences my squeal of delight by pressing his lips to mine and ravaging my mouth. My hands fly to his shoulders and I cling to him while he slams his cock into me. I moan, wanting more, as an intense pleasure twists through me.

"Oh god," I groan between kisses.

Lucas is a wild beast. He hasn't fucked me like this in years. I wrap my legs around him and try to pull him deeper as the bliss builds. I'm clawing at his back as he relentlessly fucks me.

His pace increases, and I can feel him throbbing inside me. My body shakes with each thrust as I race towards another climax. I need to come for him as much as I'm desperate for him to fill me up.

I'm chanting, "Fuck me," as we buck and thrash together. I'm mindless with need and consumed by pleasure.

He reaches a hand down to tease my clit as he growls and thrusts deep inside me. Heat streaks through me and I'm riding an almost painful edge as the tension coils in my core. The sounds of our shared passion fill the tent as my whimpers of delight join his moans of pleasure.

I ride his cock and his fingers until I can't take it anymore.

He pants, "Come for me, baby," and I come apart.

The orgasm is so powerful that it takes my breath away. My entire body goes rigid as I scream, "Yesssss!"

I squeeze my muscles around his cock and I'm wracked with shudders of pleasure. He pounds into me repeatedly until he explodes. His body jerks and I cling to him as his cock pulses deep inside me, flooding me with his warm cum.

He slows his thrusts until he stops fully. I'm dazed and can't speak. He's fucked me senseless.

Lucas rolls onto his back, taking me with him so I'm on top. I melt into him, enjoying the closeness. We're both damp from the workout. I can't resist kissing his chest and flicking my tongue out to taste him. Mmmm, I love his salty-sweet flavor after a vigorous lovemaking session.

We lay there in silence, savoring the afterglow. I'm sated and exhausted, but unwilling to move. I'm in my happy place and right where I want to be.

Lucas finally stirs and kisses the top of my head. I look up and his eyes search mine. I can tell he's assessing if everything is okay.

It takes a moment to find words again. I was fucked so thoroughly I'm a little loopy, and I giggle softly. "How was that?"

God, please say it was great.

His mouth curls into a smile. "It was amazing."

My heart leaps as I snuggle against him harder. "Good."

Neither of us seems inclined to say more, so I turn my mind off and drift in a haze of satisfaction. I relax, savoring the connection with him, until his breathing evens out and I can tell he's dozing.

Giving in to the exhaustion, I fall asleep on him.

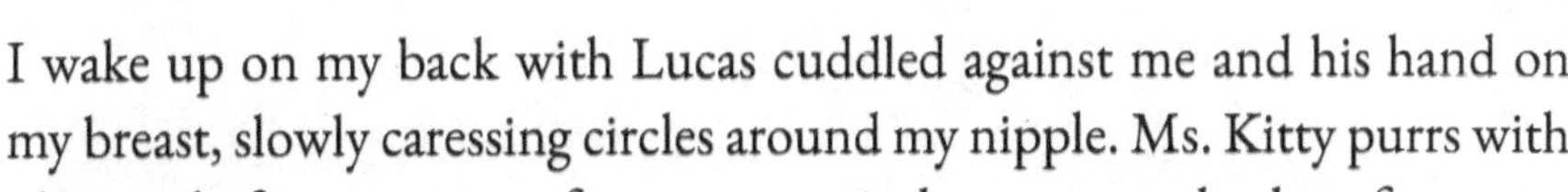

I wake up on my back with Lucas cuddled against me and his hand on my breast, slowly caressing circles around my nipple. Ms. Kitty purrs with pleasure before a twinge of soreness reminds me we need a day of rest.

"Morning," he whispers when he can tell I'm awake, and kisses my neck.

"Mmm, morning."

I bump against him, forcing him off of me so I can roll on my side and face him. He puts his arm around me and caresses my shoulder while I trace heart patterns on his chest.

His voice is still gruff from waking. "I love you, Jessica."

I lift my mouth and kiss him softly. "I love you, too."

I search his eyes and I can tell nothing has changed with him. His gaze is full of love and a deep contentment settles over me. Damn, I have the best husband in the world.

"So..." His voice holds a teasing tone. "Pleasant trip?"

I give him a delighted giggle and kiss him soundly. "Best trip ever!"

"Enough, so you'd want to do it again?"

His tone is still joking, but I can tell the question is serious. I pause and pretend to think about it for a moment before raising an eyebrow at him. "Maybe not the camping part. But we can do the other stuff at home, right?"

This is his chance to get me to be a hotwife more often. Is he going to take it?

He smiles slowly. "I think I can arrange something at home for you to enjoy."

A tingle of pleasure runs down my spine. I bury my face in his chest so he can't see the huge grin that spreads across my face, and murmur, "Sounds good."

Oh hell, yes! I am going to get more cock, and I won't even have to go camping again. My mind spins as a new world of possibility opens up for our marriage.

There's much to think about, but I push it all aside so I can enjoy this moment. I know Lucas and I have more to discuss, and I need to process what happened last night fully, but for now, this is enough.

I cuddle close to him and sigh happily. I'm more in love with my husband than ever.

The End

Sharing Her Treats

Chapter 1

It takes my brain a few moments to figure out what the annoying beep is. Groaning, I roll over and blindly fumble around the nightstand until I encounter the rubbery edges on my phone case. I crack my eyes open, swipe my alarm off, and blink at the illuminated numbers.

Ugh. I hate mornings.

The other side of the bed is empty and cold. My husband, Lucas, leaves for work by the time I wake up, which is probably for the best. I'm a grumpy bear before my morning coffee.

I force myself out of bed and stumble into the kitchen. Yawning, I notice Lucas sent me a text message.

He better not have forgotten to put the trashcan on the curb again. If I have to put shoes on, he's going to experience the full fury of my inner beast.

Lucas: You never told me what costume you're wearing tonight.

Oh right, it's Halloween. Yeah, I need coffee for this conversation. Tapping my fingers on the counter, I stare at my drip coffee maker. Could it go slower? I'll be forty by the time my drink is ready.

Fuck it. I type out my reply to Lucas.

Me: Ugh, do we have to go? My draft is due to my editor Monday.

I'm a full-time indie author and my life is pretty crazy awesome. Since I was young, I've been writing stories on whatever scraps of paper I could find. I'd spend hours daydreaming elaborate conversations between imaginary people. I loved writing, but my parents didn't think writing was a viable career, so I struggled through a business degree.

The only good thing to come out of my college years was meeting Lucas. He was a nerdy math major who was the first guy to see the "me" beyond the petite frame, generous breasts, and blonde hair. He claims he won the lotto with me, but in reality, we both won. Before him, my dating life was a string of boys. Oh, they were fun to toy with, but not worth sticking with long term.

We married right out of college. I worked boring desk jobs and wrote smutty fanfiction on breaks and in the evenings. Four years ago, I got brave enough to self-publish an erotic vampire reverse harem novel, and it blew up. I've been riding the high since, but even though I work from home, I sometimes struggle to stay on track. It's too easy to waste my day on social media or instant messaging my best friend, Miri.

Being an author is awesome, but it's not the best part of my life. No, that's Lucas. He's the most amazing man on the planet, and being in a relationship where your partner lets you be the real you is everything.

I always struggled with the idea of monogamy. One man for the rest of my life? It didn't sound appealing until I met Lucas. I wanted it all: a man at home, others when I wanted, and maybe some extra action on the side. But just because I wanted it didn't mean it was going to happen. My parents taught me that marriage means you found the last person you're ever going to fuck. In the end, I decided Lucas was worth it. I set aside my concerns about not being satisfied with one guy and said "I do" while still daydreaming of my own reverse harem.

I didn't tell Lucas about my filthy fantasies of sleeping with other men, using my writing to explore those desires. My husband is a visual creature and prefers porn to erotica, so he didn't read my stories. He didn't realize I wrote about women fucking multiple men.

A couple of years ago, I noticed our computer browser's history was full of wife sharing porno. I watched a few for research — yeah... research — and I jumped Lucas in a frenzy when he got home from work. After a round of sweaty sex and a fabulous orgasm, I questioned him about his porn preference. He admitted to having fantasies of other men fucking me.

I never imagined I would marry a man who enjoyed sharing me. Hell, I didn't even know it was an option. What followed was a wild year of sexual exploration that has settled into a comfortable, yet exciting, routine where Lucas selects men for me to fuck. My dear husband has a kink about listening to me with the other guys and imagining what is happening, so he's never in the room with us. He finds the men, invites them over, and I fuck them in our spare room. It's hot as hell to be plowed by another guy, knowing that Lucas is listening from the other side of the wall and stroking.

Dammit. Not today. Lucas won tickets to a Halloween haunted house in a work raffle, and he expects me to go with him. This is *so* not on my to-do list. I usually enjoy holidays, but I'm not feeling it this year. I didn't even buy candy to give out. My phone dings, bringing me back to my immediate problem.

Lucas: Yes, you promised. Now go figure out what you're going to wear.

Bleh. I stick my tongue out at the phone and want to have a tantrum, but I have to be an adult since I agreed to go.

Me: Fine. I'll decide after I get caffeine in me.

Lucas replies with a kissing emoji. I pout as I pour my coffee.

Dammit, why did you have to win the stupid raffle? Angst simmers in my stomach as my muscles tighten. The looming Monday deadline stresses me out, and wasting time at a haunted house doesn't help.

I drain my first cup of coffee and pour a second before taking the mug with me into our walk-in closet. Now to find a dumb costume I can recycle from past years. I dig around. Fifteen minutes later, I have three options laid out on the bed and I'm sending Miri a text. I'll let her choose.

Me: OK, I need your help with my costume. I can be a slutty nun, slutty cop, or slutty bunny.

It doesn't take long for her reply.

Miri: You should probably be a slutty something tonight.

Her message ends with an emoji of a face with its tongue sticking out. I gaze upwards and count to four slowly. I'm going to need more coffee to deal with her and Lucas today.

Me: Come on, pick for me. He's dragging me to this stupid-ass haunted house. Make my life easier.

Earlier in the week, I told her about the tickets that Lucas won. She thought it sounded fun, and I offered to let her go in my place. When she joked about fondling Lucas's ass in a dark room, I rescinded the offer. I'm assuming she was kidding, but she and her husband recently opened their marriage and she fucked a guy we went to high school with, so I wasn't sure.

Miri: OK, spoilsport. Be a slutty Jessica bunny and twitch your tail at that sexy husband of yours. Make him wish you were at home.

I narrow my eyes and tense my shoulders when she says Lucas is sexy. I realize what happened and roll them, snickering at myself. Shit, I need to lighten up. She's not trying to get with Lucas, and he is quite delicious. He was geeky in college, but he filled out and gained confidence. I've noticed women eying him when we're out shopping.

Me: Thanks, bunny it is!

Well, that's settled. Now on to important matters. Slumping my shoulders, I expel a huge, dramatic sigh as I carry my mug to the office to fix the plot hole I found in my story.

Chapter 2

Around lunch time, Lucas texted me and told me he's leaving work a few hours early and he wants me ready to leave when he gets home. Once I focused I flew through my editing, so I treated myself to a long shower and gave extra attention to grooming Ms. Kitty. If I twitch my tail enough, I'm positive I'll get a vigorous fucking once we're home.

The costume is simple. It's a relic of my college years, when I thought being a Playboy Bunny was glamorous. It's a black satin one-piece body suit with no shoulder straps that plunges so deep in the front my breasts spill over the top. The outfit zips up the back and has an attached white fluffy tail and matching rabbit ears. If I'm being honest, it's a fancy bathing suit.

I slip on a pair of black spiked heels. Yeah, it's a dumb choice for shoes, but whatever. I'm going with it.

Should I have reminded Miri what the costume looked like? We've been friends since middle school, so she saw it years ago.

Nah. I bet she would have still said to be a slutty bunny. Lucas is lucky I'm wearing a costume and not my flannel pajamas. It would've served him right if I met him at the door in my comfy PJs and announced I was going as an indie author.

Once I got more in the holiday spirit, I took the time to style my long, blonde hair in loose curls because it's Lucas's favorite. I carefully apply my makeup, and when I examine myself in the mirror, I feel sexy as all fuck. The high heels give the illusion of long legs on my five-foot-nothing frame. At thirty-three, my hips are fuller than they were in college, but the costume still fits. If anything, it might possibly look better, now that I have more to fill it. This is a delightful self-confidence boost and I'm ready to wow Lucas... and get fucked.

My phone rings when it's almost time for Lucas to get home and the lock screen says it's him.

I give a hesitant, "Hello?"

The traffic noises in the background tell me he's somewhere outside. "Hey, I stopped to get gas and I'm five minutes away. Are you ready?"

My pulse quickens with desire. Now that I'm in my slutty costume with a shaved Ms. Kitty, I really just want to stay home and fuck like rabbits. I never told Lucas what I was wearing. Will he even remember it?

I keep my voice light and flirty. "Yep, your sexy bunny is ready for you."

"Is that the costume with the black bodysuit and white tail?"

Giggling, I purr, "Maybe. You'll see when you get here."

"Hmm... No. Take a picture of yourself and send it to me. No excuses. Do it."

His command thrills me. Since I'm standing by the mirror in the bedroom, I tell him to hold on and snap a side-view photo. This way, he can appreciate my shapely ass and the bunny tail.

I send it to him. "It's on its way. You can admire my tail."

He's silent for a few seconds before he gives a husky reply. "That is very nice."

My body warms at his tone and Ms. Kitty is already wet, contemplating all the wicked things we could do later. The car chimes as he climbs in and slams the door shut. The background noise is gone, and I can hear him clearly.

"So, do you want to have a little fun tonight?"

My pussy buzzes and a flutter of pleasure runs down my legs. I know my dear husband. When he suggests "fun", it usually ends up with his cock inside me in a semi-public location. Does he want to fuck me around the back of the haunted house?

I try to sound sexy to entice him. "I'm always interested in a good time. What do you have in mind?"

I can hear the smile in his voice when he answers. "His name is Chris."

Whoa, what's this? He wants me to fuck someone named Chris. Is Chris going to be there tonight? Is this a work buddy of his?

I clench my thighs together in anticipation. The last shred of annoyance at having to go to the haunted house vanishes. "Do we know a Chris?"

He snorts. "Not yet. But you could become intimately acquainted with him tonight."

I should joke with him and tell him no, but it's pointless. He knows me too well. I have no reason to play coy.

"I think me and Ms. Kitty are *very* eager to meet Chris."

He laughs when I stress the word "very".

"OK, baby. Consider it done. I'll be there in a few minutes. I'm going to message Chris the picture of the sexy bunny he's fucking."

He signs off with, "Love you. See you in a few," and I barely have time to tell him I love him back before he ends the call. My brain whirls and I stare at my phone. Tonight just got interesting. The growing wetness between my thighs proves I'm definitely intrigued by becoming acquainted with this Chris person.

Ms. Kitty offers her approval and my pussy clenches as I daydream about being fucked by a stranger. Lucas always listens in and gets worked up, and then afterwards he unloads his pent up sexual tension on me and reminds me I'm his. I wasn't sure sex was on the menu tonight and now I'm getting two cocks. God, I really am living the dream.

Chapter 3

Lucas doesn't need much time at home since he wore his costume to work. He's dressed as a 70s hippie, and I enjoy the view of his ass in the corduroys as I follow him out to the car.

Once we're buckled in, I press him for details. "So… Is Chris a work friend, or did you meet him on the app?"

Lucas finds men for me to fuck on an app and invites them over to our house. It's been less than a handful of times I've fucked someone anywhere else, and he keeps the app a secret so I can't sneak a peek at the pool of candidates. Spoilsport.

My sweet husband is driving, and gives me a side-eye flicker as he keeps his attention on the road. "Neither."

Ugh, is he *trying* to be annoying? "Okay, so how do you know Chris?"

"Aren't you the curious bunny tonight?"

I vacillate between thoughts of punching his arm or blowing him a kiss for being so damn annoyingly cute.

I deepen my voice and try to sound threatening. "You're going to have a cranky bunny on your hands if you don't tell me how you know him."

The corners of his mouth pull up. "Let's say he's a friend of a friend, and I heard he enjoys playing with married women."

Mmm, yeah, that's an acceptable answer. I shift in the seat and wish Lucas was rubbing between my legs. I stare out the window and study the passing fields. Wherever he's taking me is a fair distance out of town, but it's not dark yet since he got off work early.

In the end, it doesn't matter how he found Chris. I trust Lucas and I'm rarely disappointed. In fact, the only time in the last year he chose badly was when he invited over a guy who showed up in assless chaps. Chappy, as I dubbed the dude, was an eager one-minute man. After Chappy apologized and left, Lucas fucked me for hours to make up for it.

The drive takes around thirty minutes and when we pull into a dirt parking lot, I'm surprised by how few cars there are for Halloween.

"Where is everyone?"

"Oh." He shrugs with feigned casualness. "The haunted house doesn't open for another hour. We're getting a semi-private tour."

My brain blips out for a moment and I consider what this might mean. Ms. Kitty adds her two cents.

Lucas stops the car and angles his body towards me. "Baby, once we're in there, if we're separated, I want you to go with it."

My eyes grow round and my pulse beats faster. "Something is happening IN the house?"

Lucas leans forward and I instinctually meet him halfway.

He brushes his lips against mine. "Nothing is going to happen you don't want. Chris knows your safe word and I'll be within hearing distance."

All my nerve endings zing. I never included a haunted house in my fantasies, but I'm totally on board with the plan.

I throw myself across the seat to give him an enthusiastic kiss. "Okay, love. Let's do this. I'm ready to get boned by a skeleton!"

He barks out a laugh as we climb out of the car. I faintly hear him mutter, "He's not a skeleton."

I don't want to know what Chris's costume is, so I don't ask for clarification. This idea of anonymous, filthy haunted house sex is the fantasy I never knew I wanted. I'm so wet my costume is going to be a mess by the end of the night. It's a good thing it'll be dark when we leave.

I slide my palm into Lucas's and we head towards a wooded path. There's a house faintly visible through the trees. I was daydreaming when Lucas told me about the haunted house, but I remember him saying it's run by an escape room company and they turn it into a haunted house for two weeks every October.

Lucas squeezes my hand and glances at me. "Are you ready?"

Desire burns a pit in my stomach, and I lick my lips. "Hell yes. Bring on the monster fucking."

Chapter 4

The path through the trees is lit by hanging lanterns. The gravel crunches under our feet and walking in heels is difficult. I have to watch the ground to make sure I don't trip. Yep, I'm an idiot. I mentally curse myself until we enter a clearing.

The house isn't one of those cheesy haunted mansions you see at carnivals. It appears to be a genuine abandoned house. Broken windows line the front with scraps of old wood slapped over the openings. Any unbroken windows are dirty, and the yard is a jungle of knee-high weeds. It has a slanted porch with damaged railings that has seen better days. The warped siding was once blue, but now it's mostly stripped of paint and chipped. This is not what I was expecting. What the fuck sort of janky business is this?

We're greeted outside by a woman in her early twenties dressed in a fairy costume with an apron tied around her waist. The semi-normal Halloween costume eases some of my concerns.

Her "Hello!" is perky, and she eyes our costumes. "A hippie and a bunny. You must be here for Chris."

I glance sharply at her as Lucas replies, "Yep."

Lucas hands her our tickets, and she slides them into a pocket of her apron with a wide smile. "You can head in. Chris said he would find you inside."

Lucas thanks the fairy, and we walk towards the house. Apprehension looms over me with each unsteady step. What are we doing here? This doesn't seem like fun times. He holds my hand to help me across the porch and I hold my complaints, trying to keep an open mind.

The door is wide open, the inside dark. My heart beats double time, and I want to turn around. I'm doubting Chris is worth this. I hate scary things. A funhouse would have been so much better.

As soon as we pass the threshold, we're immediately hit with a waft of stale air. A wall blocks the path straight in front of us and a crooked sign hangs on the wall with a double-sided arrow that states, "Pick a direction."

Lucas grins at me. "You choose."

Sure, give me the choice between two evils, so when something bad happens, it's my fault.

I shake off the thought as unworthy. Lucas is many things, but he's never set me up for anything unpleasant. I tip my head and take all of two seconds before tugging him to the left. I read somewhere that if given an option, most people choose right. Ever since then, I made it a point to go left. If fucked up shit was going to go down in a haunted house, something told me it would be to the right.

I haven't been to many haunted houses, but this one isn't like any of them. I was expecting amusement park spooky music and ghosts booing and swinging out at me, but none of that happens and it's creeping me out. They wouldn't charge if nothing happens, so I get more anxious by the second. My writers' imagination is having a field day and I'm hating every step.

We walk through a short, dirty hallway with cobwebs lining the ceiling.

Ewww, they're real.

Sticky webs line the top of the walls, and I press closer to Lucas's side. Movement out of the corner of my eye has me peering at the webbing. Shit, I think there's something up there. I swear I see something black and small moving fast behind the white wisps.

Oh, hell no!

We need to leave. A shiver runs down my spine and the hairs on the back of my neck stand up while I fight the urge to scratch all over. If a spider dropped on me, it could easily slide right down my cleavage. Yeah... this isn't sexy scary and was a bad idea. Bad, bad idea. Terrible. The worst ever.

Somehow I keep moving. The end of the hall opens up to a creepy-ass nursery. The walls are half-covered with ripped and faded wallpaper, and the room is full of broken furniture. A rocking chair in the corner moves on its own. The sound of a baby crying fills the space. I grip Lucas's hand tighter and stumble into him. It's faint and the echoes give it an eerie tone. I take deep breaths.

Chill out, Jessica. It's a recording. None of this is real.

Lucas holds my arm and I about jump straight in the air when the crib shakes. The baby blanket on the mattress balloons as if there's now a baby underneath it.

"This is scary," I moan-whisper to Lucas and keep a death grip on his hand.

His presence is the only thing keeping me from screaming and running out of here. The ghostly cry continues, louder and stronger, and the crib shakes furiously until the mattress bounces and the legs clatter against the floorboards. Um, yeah, it might be time to nope the fuck out of here.

When the rocking chair speeds up, I yank Lucas towards the door on the opposite wall. He gives no resistance as we scurry out of the fucked-up nursery. My anxiety eases slightly once we're in another short hallway. There are three doors at the end in a T pattern, so we'll have to choose our direction again. I'm *soooo* making Lucas pick this time, so I can blame him if something goes wrong.

We pause at the end and look into the room straight ahead. It's an old timey kitchen, which reassures me for a moment. Then I look up. Knives hang from the ceiling, dangling above the path leading to the doorway on the other side. Okay, that's an enormous hell no. Yep, I'm done here.

Turning to Lucas, I open my mouth to tell him we're leaving, when something from the right-hand doorway grips my arm and yanks me into the room. The door slams shut. I scream, and a warm hand covers my mouth, muffling my cries.

A werewolf holds me captive while I tremble and blink to clear my vision. I stop screaming as tiny details come into focus. It's really a dude in a costume — not that I think werewolves are real. He's wearing ripped jeans and combat boots, but from the waist up, he's furry with a full mask that obscures his face. The costume is good quality, and if I saw him in the woods, I'd run for it. I mean, hell, I'm about ready to run for it right now.

My stomach muscles tighten and blood rushes in my ears. The hand against my mouth is very much human, but a fake wolf's paw covers the backside and attaches with elastic around his palm. If his arms were at his side, he'd look as if he had furry hands with claws.

A mental image of me fucking a werewolf pops into my head and my heart hammers again, but excitement ripples through me as well. Ms. Kitty buzzes a little and I feel the heat of a blush on my face. Huh, okay. I'm not hating this idea.

When he removes his hand, he steps back and examines me quietly. Shit, am I supposed to say something?

My throat is dry, and I swallow so I can speak. "You're Chris?"

This better be Chris. Otherwise, I'm going to scream Bloody Mary again.

The werewolf nods. His voice is gruff. "Now is your chance to run away."

Run away? The decision hangs in the air for a moment.

Now that I've got my bearings and I know this is Chris, that tempting, delicious, forbidden lust burns through me and my nipples harden. God, is it fucked up that I'm getting turned on by this?

Shame and desire war inside my brain. I want him to fuck me savagely until I can't think. A delicious shudder ripples through me at the thought of us rutting like wild beasts. Oh yeah, I want this. I suppress a grin. Somehow Lucas knew and arranged it.

Stepping closer to him, I give him a sultry smile. "Do your worst."

Okay, maybe I shouldn't have said that. Lust zings straight to my pussy and I get a slutty, naughty thrill. I'm getting off on this way more than I would have thought.

The werewolf nods but doesn't speak as he steps closer. He twists me around and shoves me against the nearest wall, smashing my breasts against the rough plaster.

I gasp, "Oh," as he yanks down the zipper of my costume.

Shit, I guess we're starting. I had a few scenarios in my head of how tonight might play out, and being used by a werewolf wasn't one I considered. I mean, it's awesome, but still...

A thud on the floor startles me and I glance down. The werewolf mask's empty eyes stare at me. Uh oh. In every horror movie I've watched, if you see the evil guy's face, you're a goner. This better not be a horror erotica movie.

Despite how fucked up this is, the hint of danger is turning me into a needy mess. Wet heat flares between my legs and I imagine myself on my knees, sucking his cock. A terrible hunger crawls into my brain and I want to beg him to use me however he wants.

Chris yanks the top of my costume down, exposing my breasts to the cool air. He tugs the fabric over my curvy hips until it drops to the floor. I step one foot out so I don't get tangled in it and trip. Removing that one piece leaves me naked, since I'm not wearing panties or a bra. Ms. Kitty gets even wetter at the harsh treatment as wild, raw need flutters in my core.

When he grinds against my ass and my nipples scrape the plaster, I moan from the intense pleasure-pain. He's nice and hard through his jeans, and a switch flips in my brain. Everything is now erotic instead of scary. I'm loving every minute of this.

I moan as he kisses the back of my neck and rasps, "Has a werewolf ever bred you?"

My brain freezes for a split second.

Holy fuck.

I'm not in a horror movie. This is one of my motherfucking novels. Or nearly so. It would have been vampire breeding if I wrote it, but you can bet your ass I'm going to write a filthy werewolf story after this.

I moan loudly. "No, I haven't."

He brings his hands around to my breasts and tugs on my nipples. He continues to rub against my ass and the friction of his jeans increases my need to have a cock inside me.

No one said I had to pretend to fight, and I'd rather play easy to get. "Mmmm, I'm ready for breeding."

My novels always have kick-ass women who embrace the weird shit that happens to them, so if this is my novel, my protagonist would plead for a hard breeding.

He stops playing with my tits and forces my legs apart with his knee. I adjust my position to give him better access as he glides his hand down the curve of my ass cheek, caressing me. He slides his fingers against my pussy and grazes my wet folds. It's enough to drive me crazy.

He's teasing me and doesn't press his finger in. "I'm not sure my bunny is ready to be bred yet. I think she needs to be stroked some more."

Lucas is probably laughing his ass off at this dirty talk... or maybe not. He's probably stroking his cock and imagining all of this.

"Whatever you want." I groan as he presses a finger into my wetness and seeks my clit.

"Yes," he growls. "It is whatever I want."

He rubs circles on my clit, and a shock of pleasure consumes me. "Oh, fuck."

A gush of wetness coats his hand, and I arch against him as he continues to tease my swollen bundle of nerves. His warm breath on my neck thrills me, and I'm transported when he growls and bites my shoulder. He doesn't do it hard enough to break the skin, but it's going to leave a mark.

This is more like it.

I embrace the fantasy. I close my eyes and imagine he's still wearing the mask. I'm bent over a log in a forest, not imagining an actual werewolf, but the idea of a guy in a costume breeding me in the woods hits a kink I didn't know I had.

He continues to fondle me with one hand. My breathing speeds up at the sound of his zipper. When his bare cock presses between the cleft of my buttcheeks, I moan as my pussy throbs with pleasure. He shoves me closer to the wall. I have to turn my head and put the side of my face against the cold plaster. My moans get louder as he slides the tip of his cock up and down my wet folds, not pressing in... not giving me what I crave.

A forbidden hunger makes me whimper. "Oh god, fuck me... Please."

His voice rumbles in my ear. "Oh no, my bunny isn't warmed up enough yet."

The way he keeps saying "My bunny" has a possessive naughtiness to it. I'm Lucas's bunny, but the more Chris repeats it, the more I want to be his as he fucks and breeds me.

He plays "just the tip" with my pussy. A ripple of bliss swirls in my core every time I think he's finally going to plunge all the way in. I mewl in displeasure. Fuck, I need his cock NOW.

After several agonizing short thrusts, when he pulls out again, I cry out. "No, please, you can feel how wet your bunny is."

He growls. "We'll see."

He yanks me away from the wall and drags me over to an old dressing table with a cracked oval mirror. Chris forces my head to the surface and I catch a quick glimpse of him in the mirror before my face presses against the dusty table top.

Wow, he's cute. He has pleasant features with dark, wavy hair. With the brief look, I don't think I could pick him out of a crowd if I saw him again, but he's not going to get tossed out of anyone's bed for eating cookies and getting crumbs on the sheets.

He doesn't ask me to, but I spread my legs as wide as I can. Since we're now across the room, I don't know how well Lucas can hear us. I'm going to need to moan louder for his enjoyment. The way my head is facing, I can see a four-poster bed with ratty blankets on it and I'm glad he didn't drag me there. Yeah, no one wants to fuck on that bed. Being bent over this dirty table is much better.

This entire encounter is filthy, figuratively and literally, and I'm so on board with it. Miri won't believe the night I'm having. Hell, maybe this would've been her if I had given her my ticket.

A sharp slap on my ass snaps me to attention. "Shit."

The sting lingers as he presses his cock between my ass cheeks, placing pressure against a hole I wasn't expecting him to use. Um, this dude doesn't have lube. Fear lances my gut, but at the same time my pussy clenches in delight. This is exactly why I can't trust Ms. Kitty. She's all down with me getting ass fucked with no lube.

I'm about to protest when he shifts his position and drives straight into my pussy, drilling straight to my core.

"Ohhhhh my god." I groan from an intense spike of pleasure.

His cock is massive, much bigger than Lucas, and I feel deliciously ripped apart. My head reels as he withdraws and slams into me again, setting a punishing pace.

"You like being bred by a werewolf?" he asks in a deep roar.

"Yes," I gasp. "Fuck me harder."

I don't know why this absurd dirty talk is doing it for me, but every time he mentions breeding, I want to reply with disgusting things I've never said before... things I've never even thought about. I want to beg him to fill me with his seed, and put a baby in me. Tell him to fill my fertile womb.

I close my eyes and groan at my vulgar thoughts, and a warmth steals over me. A growing acceptance of my inner slut being unleashed sinks me into submission. He can do whatever he wants to me.

He laughs darkly, as if he can sense I've given up control. "I plan to breed you until you're a wet puddle and my seed is dripping out of you."

He takes a fistful of my hair and yanks my head back, growling as he slams into me repeatedly. I grip the sides of the vanity for leverage and my breasts scrape the surface, sending pings of bliss straight to my clit. His enormous cock feels spectacular as he stretches me wide. Jesus Christ, this is crazy and hot.

My arms shake from holding on as he rams forward, plunging himself inside me over and over again. My moans grow louder as every thrust brings me closer to the edge. I usually rub my clit to help me come, but this guy's girth massages every inch of my cave walls and I'm going to come without any added help.

I need to see how raunchy this looks, so I open my eyes and stare into the broken mirror. His head is thrown back, and he's holding onto my hips with one hand and my hair with the other as he jackhammers into me. He didn't take off the chestpiece of his costume and his hands still have the fur covering. It's a half werewolf, half human fucking me. Holy fuck, this is depraved.

My brain melts at the obscene visual and it catapults me over the edge. "Ohhhh, god!"

My back arches at the peak of my orgasm. Ripples of rapture shoot from my fingers to my toes, focusing on the nerve endings stretched around his massive tool. Waves of pleasure wash over me as he pants and fucks me harder.

I'm chanting "Fuck me" as the ecstasy spirals through me. What few thoughts I have outside the sensations blowing my mind are all about Lucas, standing in the hallway with his cock in his hand. He should have been in the room watching. This might be a once-in-a-lifetime fuck.

The bliss builds again, and just when I'm about to come for a second time, Chris shouts in pure male pleasure and explodes, coating me with his seed. He spasms against me, fucking his cum back into me for several seconds as I quiver underneath him.

When he's finished pumping, he releases my hips with a loud grunt. A stream of hot cum pours out of my pussy and coats my thighs as he pulls out. His huge cock twitches as it empties itself and leaves a trail down my legs. My legs tremble from the tickling sensation and I have the urge to taste him. I realize I'd have to let go of the vanity to do that and I'd probably collapse to the floor, so I put it from my mind.

He slumps over me, putting his palms flat on the surface to hold his weight, and presses his head against my shoulder. We stay still for several moments until his heavy breathing slows. I watch him in the mirror as I process. I'm a mess and in desperate need of a shower since he's been fucking me against dirty surfaces.

When his eyes meet mine in the mirror, they're dark with satisfaction and full of wonderment.

"Thank you, Jessica."

"You're welcome." I'm uncertain what else to say. I should probably thank him as well.

As he straightens up, his gaze drops to my thighs, smeared with his warm, sticky cum. I fight the urge to rub my thighs together, and he holds onto my upper arm to steady me as I stand. His arms wrap around me from behind, cupping my breasts with each hand. He skims his thumb across my nipples in an intimate gesture that sends tingles through me. He places a soft kiss on top of my hair, and I'm surprised by the intimate gesture.

"Your husband is waiting for you."

I give him a hazy smile. "I need to get dressed."

His soft chuckle reminds me he's only a guy in a costume, no matter how much he rocked my world and possibly gave me a new kink. He drops his hands from my breasts and gets my costume from the floor. I shimmy into it. Chris zips up the back and plays with the bunny tail. I really need to thank him, but anything I could say seems inadequate.

I can't simply walk out, so I have to try. "Thank you, Chris. This was... fucking magnificent."

Instead of responding, he flashes me a wide smile and a dimple appears in his cheek.

Oh hell, that's adorable.

And memorable. I'd probably be able to pick him out of a crowd now that I've gotten a better look at him. Lucas never picks the same guy twice, so is the only time I'll ever see him.

Dammit. This is one time I wish Lucas would change his rule.

My body is cooling down, and I shiver as his cum dries on my thighs. I peer around the room, wishing there was something I could clean with. When I see Chris again, he's slipped his werewolf mask on.

"Have a good night, Jessica." It's muffled, almost a growl, like he's back into werewolf mode, and he heads into the hallway before I can reply.

Lucas steps into the room and approaches me cautiously. My heart catches in my throat and I want to rush to him. I'm a mass of confusion at how hot that was, and I'm silent as Lucas draws me towards him, encircling me with his arms. He cups my face and his thumb caresses my lips before he kisses me tenderly.

"Are you okay?"

I nod, not trusting myself to speak.

He presses a gentle kiss on my forehead before pulling away. "Listening to him talk about breeding you was hot."

A quick glance at the bulge in his jeans confirms his words. Oh yeah, he liked it.

I can't help myself and I stroke his hardness through the fabric. "Lucas, you really should have been watching."

He groans. "Let's go home. I want to fuck you."

God, I love this man.

I tease him. "Yes please. I want your magnificent cock breeding my pussy and filling me with your seed."

His eyes glitter and he gives a delighted laugh. "I'll do whatever I want to you."

Mmmm, now this is why I married him.

Chapter 5

As soon as the front door closes behind us, Lucas shoves me against the wall and kisses me deeply, grinding his cock against my stomach. Looks like the car ride didn't cool his ardor. He slides his arms around me and unzips my bodysuit, pulling it down to expose my breasts. His hands move to cup them and my nipples tighten in response. My ping of lust wakes up Ms. Kitty, who clearly informs me she's ready for more action.

"Fuck," he growls as his mouth moves to my neck, nibbling and sucking on my skin. "I love your tits."

He takes one of my nipples into his mouth and sucks hard, making me gasp. I hope he doesn't want something long and drawn out, because I need him inside me. Soon. Sooner.

He pulls away, leaving me wanting more. Desire rips through me as he crushes his mouth to mine and kisses me while undressing himself. He separates enough to rip his shirt off before returning to my lips. Once he sheds the rest of his clothes, he grabs my hand and forces me towards the kitchen.

I fumble for a few steps before kicking my high heels off. My bodysuit is still halfway on, with my breasts bare. Lucas notices and pushes me against the edge of the table as he drags the costume down my hips.

"Spread your legs," he commands, and I immediately open them.

My inner thighs are crusted with another man's cum, but Lucas doesn't care. The table edge digs into me as he pushes two fingers inside my pussy. I'm dripping all over his hand as he pumps them in and out, and I sigh at how incredible it feels.

"Jessica...?"

"Mmmm, yes?" I wish it was his cock sliding into me instead of his fingers, but this is a start. Ms. Kitty approves.

"Ask me to fuck you. I want to hear you say it."

Squirming, I moan louder and embrace the sluttiness of what we're doing. "Oh god, please fuck me. I need your cock inside me. Please."

Removing his fingers from my pussy, he shoves me onto the kitchen table until I'm lying on my back. I'm dizzy with need as I spread my legs. Hell yeah, It's time for his cock. Let the fun begin.

Again.

My relief is short-lived as he slips his fingers back inside me. Why won't he give me his cock? He stands over me, one hand on my knee, holding them apart while he finger fucks me.

"Fuuuuck!" I writhe against his hand as the pleasure builds in my core. "Just fuck me, please!"

Lucas laughs and shakes his head as he moves the kitchen chair over so he can sit between my legs. He pulls me towards him and cups my pussy with both hands and spreads my lips, exposing my clit. His tongue glides over the sensitive nub, making me squeal.

"Are you sure?" His hot breath on my clit drives me wild and I squeal again. My hips buck, and he uses his free hand to guide them. He slides his fingers inside me to gather moisture, then rubs them together and places the wet tips against my asshole. I whimper at his touch and he raises his head to grin wickedly at me.

"Or maybe you want this tonight?"

I'm reminded of Chris, and how I half wanted him to fuck my ass, and my ready protest when I thought he was going to do it. But this is Lucas, not Chris, and I love him dearly. Lucas can do whatever he wants as long as I get his cock inside one of my holes.

Lucas spits on his finger and uses the lubrication from my pussy and his saliva to slide his finger gently into my ass. There's a moment of discomfort, but I relax and revel in the sensation. When he pushes it deeper, I cry out from pleasure. A second finger follows, stretching me wide and filling me. He pumps them in and out slowly, making sure I feel every inch.

"Is this what my slutty wife wants tonight?"

"Yes, this... yes." I whimper as he fingers my ass.

He pulls them out completely, and I mewl in disappointment. Why did he stop?

"You forgot something." I raise my head and see his wicked grin. "It's my choice, and I want your pussy."

He stands, and I groan as he pushes his thick cock all the way inside my pussy until he bottoms out.

"Oh, fuck..." Swirls of bliss make me groan and writhe as I try to buck against him.

"You like this cock?"

"Oh god, yes. I love it. I can't get enough of it."

Whenever I fuck other men, he needs to hear how much I love his cock... and I really do. Other men may fuck me, but Lucas owns me, body and soul.

He pulls almost all the way out before slamming deep inside me, the motion bringing me to the brink of orgasm. The best thing about what Lucas and I do is no matter how slutty I am, he still loves me and wants me. I get to experience my most depraved fantasies and come home to be reclaimed by the man who accepts every facet of me.

Everything I've done tonight rolls through my mind — being pretend bred by a guy I don't know, my husband's fingers in my ass, and now I'm begging for his cock — and my brain shuts off.

The room fills with the sounds of wet slapping as he hammers into me, and uncontrolled words tumble out of my mouth. "Oh, god, yes! Give it to me. I want to come all over your cock."

I need to watch his face as he cums inside me. It's so fucking hot. I'm so turned on I can barely breathe.

He growls, "You're such a dirty slut," as he slams into me.

"Yes, yes, I am." He whacks against my pussy harder.

"Do you want to come for me?"

"Yes," I pant. "Please, let me come."

He bucks his hips and moves a hand to hold my hip tightly, keeping me from rolling off the table. With his other hand, he rubs my clit. I can't believe how good he makes me feel. He's always there for me, always willing to take care of my needs and make sure I'm satisfied. I groan as he fucks me and applies pressure to my swollen bean. Energy builds in my core and my thigh muscles tighten.

"Oh god, I'm going to come," I cry out.

"Tell me you want my cum."

The room spins and I try to focus. "I want your cum, please."

He thrusts harder, and his finger against my clit speeds up. I finally tip over the edge, and scream his name and arch my back as rapture courses through me. I struggle to keep my eyes open and locked onto his as I ride the waves of bliss. He gives a final hard whack and moans passionately as he climaxes. His eyes glaze with lust as he jerks against me, unloading his seed.

I'm in a daze as the ripples of pleasure become faint shivers of delight. He stays inside me until he softens before he pulls me into a sitting position and wraps his arms around me.

"That was amazing," he whispers and kisses my forehead.

We hold each other close, basking in the afterglow of our orgasms. I might be embarrassed tomorrow when I think back to the crazy, over-the-top shit we said tonight in the heat of the moment, but hopefully it will help me write my werewolf breeding story.

As my mental fuzziness fades, I look down at his chest. He's covered with streaks of grime that he got from me.

I laugh and kiss him. "Maybe next time you'll give me the chance to clean up before you fuck me?"

"Hmm... maybe."

Maybe my ass. There's no way he'll *ever* let me shower before reclaiming me. My wonderful husband loves it when I'm a dirty slut.

The End

Sharing His Eager Hotwife

Chapter 1

Husband Chooses a Massive Guy to Fuck His Needy Hotwife

"What do you think about this one?"

My husband, Lucas, is sitting at the other end of the couch and he tips his phone at me. On the screen is a smoking hot shirtless guy wearing a cowboy hat, and I fight the urge to lick my lips. Lucas has been searching on an app for casual hook-ups for the past 15 minutes, trying to select the perfect guy for me to fuck tonight. Since he keeps tempting me with pictures of sexy men and telling me what I could do with them, I'm a turned on, wet mess. Thinking about the guy in the picture, I immediately imagine running my hands over his chest and kissing down his abs. Moisture leaks from my pussy at the thought–yeah, my panties are going to be shot after this.

I like to play a game where I pretend I'm not impressed with the guy, so I keep my tone neutral. "Uh, a cowboy? Nah, not interested."

I'm pretty sure Lucas knows the game because the more indifferent I sound, the more he tries to tempt me. I nonchalantly pluck cat hair off my yoga pants and struggle to hold back a smile when he gives his reasoning.

"But Jessica, you could ride your own cowboy." He glances at me and wiggles his eyebrows in a stupid but loveable way. "And we both know how much you like being on top."

I blow him a kiss. "Yes, but I rode you last night. I want something different."

"Hmm...." He goes back to searching on the app and I consider sliding a hand down my pants to stroke my clit. It's so fucking hot when he chooses the guy he wants me to fuck. The longer it takes, the more turned on I'm getting. When my pussy clenches and buzzes with need, I decide to go for it. I need to release some of this tension, and Ms. Kitty needs a finger inside her at the very least.

Only the tips of my fingers are under the elastic waistband of my pants when he exclaims, "Found him!"

I lean towards him, trying to peek at his phone. "Oh?"

He draws his phone away from my inquisitive eyes. "Oh, yes. You'll see tonight."

Oh fuck, he's not going to show me! A wave of lust washes over me and my entire body tingles. It's going to be a long wait until tonight.

⚬

When the doorbell rings, I'm sitting on the edge of the king-sized bed in our spare room wearing sheer, ruffled babydoll lingerie that shows everything. It's light pink with black polka dots, and molds around my breasts. My dusty-pink nipples stand out through the fabric, and the matching panties don't hide the fact I'm fully waxed below. The full-length mirror on the wall across from the bed validates that I look as sexy as I feel. My blonde, wavy hair is in a braid and I toy with the end while I wait eagerly.

Lucas and I came up with several rules for our playtimes. He invites the men over to our house so that he can meet them first and assess whether he's going to allow them to fuck me. Our home office is one room over and he waits in there, listening, while I get fucked. This way he's close if something goes wrong and I'm secure knowing he's watching out for me, even if he's not in the room.

But honestly, we've yet to meet a bad guy. I'm a firm believer that most people in this world are decent, and these guys just want to fuck a hotwife. They're looking for sexual release and I'm more than willing to give it to them.

Since the bedroom door is open I can hear their voices in the living room but not what they are saying. Their laughter echoes down the hall and gets louder as Lucas and whoever he's bringing with him head in my direction. My breath catches in anticipation and I rub my thighs together. Lucas walks in first and a massive, muscular, tattooed guy lumbers behind him. My eyes widen and I'm speechless for a moment. This guy is a giant. Did Lucas hook me up with a bodybuilder?

I'm on the petite side and this guy might cleave me in two with a powerful thrust. My brain blips out while I picture him behind me, pounding away at my pussy. My pulse speeds up and I feel like my insides are vibrating while my body flushes from neediness.

I come back to my senses when Lucas makes the introduction.

"Jessica, this is Hank."

I have to hold in my giggle. He's Hank the Tank. Realizing I need to say something before it becomes awkward, I smile sweetly at Hank.

"It's nice to meet you."

Hank is standing halfway behind Lucas, so I can't see his full crotch area. I'm curious what he's packing because I know it's a myth that big guys have large cocks. I don't think it'll matter what size he is. My body is responding to his bulk and the knowledge he could pick me up and toss me around easily. There are so many sexual positions I could do with this guy. He could be my jungle gym and fuck me while holding me midair without needing to brace me against the wall.

God, my husband is so awesome. I enjoy being held down and feeling helpless during sex, so he probably saw this dude's picture and knew I'd love his strength.

Lucas grins at me. "Right, so I'll leave you guys alone. Have fun!"

As Lucas leaves, I notice he's sporting an erection. He better not stroke to the point of coming while listening to us. I want him ready for me afterwards. The best thing about fucking other men is the amazing sex Lucas and I have after they leave. I always get a minimum of two orgasms — one from each guy — and my pussy is hoping for three tonight.

The bedroom door closes, and as Hank approaches me, I stand up. He's easily over six feet tall to my five-feet-nothing, and I contemplate climbing up on the bed to kiss him. Hank takes care of our height difference problem by bending over to brush his lips against mine. When he deepens the kiss, my pussy hums and I realize Hank hasn't said a word to me. I know he can talk because he was laughing with Lucas. Is he the strong and silent type in the bedroom?

His mouth tastes minty as we twirl our tongues, and a bolt of desire runs through me. Since I've been wet and needy all day, I need his cock inside me now. Hank takes his time with the kiss and when he makes no move to touch me, I take one of his enormous hands and put it on my breast. He teases the nipple through the sheer fabric and I moan and sway towards him as pleasure flutters in my core.

Again, he seems in no rush as he cups both my breasts and rolls my nipples between his thumbs and index fingers. It's not like I've done hundreds of one-night stands, but so far in my hotwife experiences it's not common for the guy to want to savor the experience. The guys Lucas has chosen for me all seem to want to bang furiously, almost as if they're afraid something is going to stop them before they come. I'm always halfway to my orgasm before they even get to the house, so a quickie easily tips me over the edge. But this guy is different.

Hank kisses down my neck, flicking his tongue against my skin, and I want to suggest we lie down on the bed before his back hurts from being bent over, but his mouth and tiny bit of stubble on his cheeks and chin make my head whirl. My pussy aches and I try to clear my head enough to take control and move this forward. Ms. Kitty will not wait all night and Lucas is probably wondering what the hell is going on because we're so quiet. I'm not giving him my usual vocal entertainment.

I finally can't take it any longer, and put a hand on Hank's firm chest. I almost get distracted and want to explore with my hands, but that won't get his cock in me any faster. My attempts to shove him away from me are pointless. He's unmovable, so I switch tactics.

"Hank," I purr at him, "I want you to fuck me."

God, please, just shove your cock in me before I beg. He doesn't respond but sweeps me up into his arms. I gasp and throw my arms around his neck, and my body tingles. Holy fuck, I was right. He could toss me around if he wanted. He climbs onto the bed with me and I assume he's going to try cuddling and kissing some more because this muscular dude seems to be a teddy bear... a silent teddy bear.

When he rolls me onto my stomach and props himself up on an elbow, I'm perplexed. What's going on here? His lack of talking is arousing me further. I don't know what he's thinking or what he plans to do. I moan out when he caresses my ass cheeks through my panties, and I wiggle my bum at him to encourage him to continue.

Instead, he peels my panties down to my knees. To help him remove them, I bend my legs and he easily drags them off. They are a wisp of fabric so I don't hear them fall to the floor and I can't tell what he did with them, but it doesn't matter. Ms. Kitty knows she's closer to getting stuffed, and wetness leaks out of me.

He shifts his position on the bed and I glance over my shoulder to see he's on his knees. He tugs on my legs to pull them open, and I help him by spreading them. If he wants access to my pussy, I'm going to help him in any way I can.

He rubs my ass briefly again, and when his thick fingers slip between my velvety folds and brush against my clit, I groan loudly. "Oh, god. Please fuck me. Please?"

I can tell I'm a minute away from begging, but when he rubs circles around my clit, all thoughts drain from my head. I'm a bundle of repressed energy waiting to explode, and bolts of lightning shoot through my core.

He speeds up his caressing and I cry out, "Ooooh, god," loud enough that I know Lucas can hear it through the walls. Having my husband listening in always makes me want to put on a good show.

When Hank dips a finger in my pussy, I buck against his hand and try to rise on my knees to give myself leverage to fuck his finger myself. A firm hand on my ass makes it so I can't move. The brief moment of helplessness as I fight against the pressure and realize he can pin me down with one hand makes me hit the boiling point.

I whimper, growing louder by the end of my begging. "God, I need your cock. Please fuck me? You see how wet I am? I need your cock. Please... PLEASE?"

The bed dips as he moves between my legs. When he fits the head of his cock against my pussy, I remember I never saw his package. He presses in slowly, and it only takes a moment for me to realize his cock is as massive as his body.

"Ooooooh, fuck," I cry out as my cave walls stretch and mold around him. My body zings with intense pleasure. This guy's cock might be the biggest I've ever had, and I've had some pretty massive ones recently.

I keep expecting him to haul me up on my knees, but he covers my body with his and presses me down into the bed. I guess this is how he's going to fuck me. When he bottoms out, I groan, but it turns into a squeal of delight when he pulls out fully and immediately drills straight to my core again.

I start chanting, "Oh... my... god," in a rising crescendo as he fucks me with small thrusts, hammering against a sensitive spot deep inside my pussy.

The bed springs squeak rhythmically and he's breathing heavily, but I can tell he's in shape and this isn't strenuous for him in the slightest. The room spins and I close my eyes as the ecstasy builds.

When the muscles in my body tense, I can tell I'm going to explode at any moment. All I can think about is the pleasure, and I hear myself crying out, "Fuck me," repeatedly as a tidal wave of rapture builds.

When Hank changes the tempo and switches to long strokes, it tips me over the edge.

"Ooooh, god!" I practically scream as my orgasm smacks me in the face.

I shudder and quake under him, and my pussy massages his cock as I ride the waves of the intense orgasm. Every nerve ending in my body sings and I don't know how long it all lasts because every thrust of his keeps my climax going. When he speeds up and grinds against my pussy, I can tell he's about to come.

When he finally explodes, he cries out, and his warm cum coats my walls. I shiver with aftershocks of pleasure and he fucks his cum inside me for a few more strokes. He rolls to the side and stretches out on the bed next to me. I smile at him, still dazed from the bliss, and he tenderly strokes the side of my face.

"Thank you, Jessica."

His voice is deep, and my grin widens. Finally hearing him speak thrills me. His cum drips out of me, and I revel in the feeling. This isn't the only load of cum I'm getting tonight, and the thought of Lucas draining his balls in me revs my pussy back to life.

God, I love my life.

The End

Chapter 2

Husband Chooses the Perfect Guy to Give His Hotwife a Hard Pounding

My husband, Lucas, has a twinkle in his hazel eyes when I walk in the door from my weekend at a luxury spa resort. "I've got a surprise for you, Jessica."

Abandoning the handle of my wheeled suitcase, I wrap my arms around him and kiss him deeply. As our tongues swirl together, I detect a hint of chocolate—mmm, yummy. The entire flight home I thought about fucking him, and I'm wet and horny. He told me to expect a hard pounding when I walked in the door and it's been three days since we've fucked. I don't want to wait any longer.

When I press against his growing erection, I can't help but smile. I'm not the only impatient one. Stroking him through the fabric of his jeans, I moan while I imagine him sliding inside me. I spent the weekend on self care so I'm relaxed, fully waxed, and ready for action.

He chuckles and breaks off the kiss. "Aren't you curious about the surprise?"

Taking a step backwards, I lift the edge of my pink T-shirt over my head and ponytail, exposing my white lace bra, and drop it on the hardwood floor. "You can tell me while you're fucking me."

Unhooking my bra, I slide it down my arms and it joins the shirt on the floor. As my full, perky breasts bounce free, I groan with relief and massage the firm globes with my hands, toying with my nipples. I'm turning myself on even more and he better not make me wait long.

Lucas looks amused as I kick my sneakers off and drag my leggings and underwear down. I'm not sure what's so funny. He obviously hasn't realized I mean business. I WILL have his cock inside me. He better plan on giving me the pounding he promised.

"Well?" I toss my head in challenge once I'm fully naked. The ends of my blonde hair brush against my shoulders, causing a delicious shiver to run through me.

His lust-filled gaze sweeps down to the shaved Ms. Kitty, and he licks his lips. My pulse races and my pussy throbs as if all the blood was rushing straight to it. Whenever one of us is gone for a few days, it's always like this. They say distance makes the heart grow fonder, and in our marriage, it seems to be true. I want to fuck his brains out right here, right now.

Lucas holds out a hand to me, and I slide my palm into his. He gives me a sly grin. "You know that hard pounding I promised you?"

I raise my eyebrows at him. "Yeah..."

A tingle runs up my arm when he kisses the back of my hand, and his eyes crinkle with a smile. "I never said it was going to be from me."

Oooooh, what's this? My nipples harden while my pussy clenches. "There's a guy here right now?"

He laughs out a, "Yes," and tugs my hand. "He's waiting for you in the spare room. You ready for him?"

Lucas enjoys choosing guys for me to fuck, but this is something new. He's never had someone on standby when I got home. Moisture trickles down my thigh as he leads me down the hall. Whenever we have someone over to fuck me, my husband always stays in our home office. He can listen through the adjoining wall, stroke himself, and also be close for safety.

This situation piques my curiosity. What type of guy did my husband choose for me this time? Lucas enters the spare room first, and steps to the side so I can see the guy. He's standing by the window and smiles when he sees me. He's fairly unremarkable—average build, brown hair that needs a trim—not the typical guy Lucas chooses. I'm surprised by his casual clothes. He's wearing basketball shorts, a T-shirt, and he's barefoot. How long has he been here?

"Jessica, this is Owen."

My sharp, questioning glance must have been obvious, because Lucas continues. "Owen came highly recommended."

I hold in a snort. Who's he getting recommendations from? Was he on a website for people seeking bulls to fuck their hotwife?

Owen clears his throat and his voice is deeper than I expected. "Wow, you're gorgeous."

I realize I'm greeting this guy naked, and his compliment thrills me. I decide to let go of any misgivings. Lucas had a reason for asking this guy over and I trust my husband. Plus, if he turns out to be a dud, Lucas will finish me off.

I smile softly at Owen. "It's nice to meet you."

Lucas kisses my cheek. "I'll be next door. Have fun."

As he leaves, he smacks my ass and I squeak while a bolt of pleasure zips through me. He shuts the door behind him and I'm uncertain what to do next.

Owen walks over to me and holds out both his hands, palms up. I didn't notice it before, but his hands are enormous. I'm petite, and as I slide my hands in his, they engulf mine. A tingle of delight makes my breath catch as I imagine those massive paws on my tits. Suddenly I'm desperate for his cock. My pussy buzzes, and I almost giggle. Ms. Kitty is eager to get started as well.

He tugs me against him, wrapping an arm around my waist and using the free hand to cup my face as he kisses me. At first it's just a soft brush of the lips, but when he applies pressure, I open my mouth and welcome his tongue with light flicks of my own. As the kiss deepens and we press together, his thin shorts hide nothing and I notice that, even if his appearance is pretty average, his erect cock isn't.

He slowly pushes me towards the bed as I slide my hands under his shirt, caressing his chest and running my fingers through his chest hair. I'm delighted and want to touch him all over to see if he's got this much hair anywhere else. It's not like he's a beast, but Lucas is practically hairless so I'm intrigued. He pauses for a moment to take off his shirt, tosses it to the floor, and claims my mouth again. He's a wonderful kisser and I'm getting wetter by the minute. God, this is so damn hot and Lucas is so fucking amazing for arranging this. He's giving up the chance to fuck me right now, knowing it's going to drive me wild and we'll most likely have amazing sex later. But this still means he's waiting in sexual agony, stroking himself and listening to my moans.

"Did your husband tell you anything about me?"

I stop kissing him and search his face. What didn't Lucas tell me? "No...."

He smirks at me, states, "Good," and forces me backwards onto the mattress, catching me right before I'd fall and lowering me carefully. He crawls up next to me while I adjust my position to the center of the bed. His gaze sweeps up and down my full length, and I fight the urge to squirm.

He kisses me briefly and whispers in his soothing deep tone, "Close your eyes."

I obey and my breath catches as he explores my body with his mouth and his hands, as if he's trying to memorize every curve. He kisses down my chest, avoiding my nipples, and flicks his tongue in little circles as if he's tasting me as he works his way to my belly button and back up. When he latches into one of my nipples, I moan and arch against him as swirls of ecstasy ignite my core. He continues to suck on the tip, playing with the opposite breast with his other hand. Twin spikes of pleasure zing straight to my clit. Fuuuck, I need something inside me, preferably his cock, but even his fingers would do at this point.

Everything feels wonderful and keeping my eyes closed heightens the pleasure. I don't know what to expect, and I'm still not sure what's extra special about him. Even though his cock seemed large through his shorts, I've been with larger men. No matter the size, I still want him and he needs to shove it in me.

When he runs his hand down my legs and tugs up on them, I bend my knees, putting my feet flat on the bed. He caresses my calves and inner thighs, getting close to my pussy but never touching it. The longer he avoids the apex of my legs, the needier I become and wetness runs down my crack. If he doesn't give me what I want soon, he's going to make me beg.

When he finally brushes his fingers along my pussy lips, I moan and spread my knees wider. He's not pressing in and only using a light, teasing caress along my shaved skin.

The tickling sensation finally makes me groan, "Oh god, please fuck me."

A thick digit glides along my folds and presses in, brushing against my clit gently. I moan and thrash my head from the intense pleasure, but I need more.

I cry out in desperation, "Please, please, please, will you fuck me? I need your cock so bad."

He pulls his hand away, and I moan in protest. The gentle rubbing was driving me crazy, but having nothing against me is worse. I keep my eyes closed while he shifts on the bed, and I can tell he's removing his shorts. Oh, thank God. This means he's finally going to fuck me.

Positioning himself between my bent knees, he slowly presses his cock into me and I can't hold back my loud moan. He's thicker than I expected and my tightness molds around him. He gives me time to adjust to his size and when he's fully ensheathed into my warm, wet pussy, he pauses and leans forward to kiss me some more. I buck up against him, forcing the head of his cock to rub deep inside and causing electricity to spread from my core.

"Jessica, tell me what you want," he demands between kisses.

I'm feeling slutty and desperate, so I don't hesitate. "Fuck me hard and fast. I need it rough."

Owen nibbles down my neck and back to my breast. He sucks on a nipple for a moment and then takes it between his teeth and tugs on it, giving me an amazing, painful pleasure. "Oh, god," I moan and try to shift against his cock, desperate for gratification.

He releases my nipple from his teeth and chuckles. "Your husband said you liked it rough."

Mmm, Lucas enjoys orchestrating what happens with the men and it doesn't surprise me he gave Owen pointers. "Yes," I pant out, hoping this means he'll give me what I want.

"Good." Owen says and withdraws his cock from me as I peep out in distress.

Jesus Christ, this guy needs to fuck me. I can't handle this exquisite torture.

A strong lunge straight to my core has me crying out, and my eyes fly open as Owen hammers against my pussy. "Ooooh, fuck," I moan loudly as I meet his every thrust. His thickness caresses every nerve ending I have inside me, and my back arches as I try to get him as deep as I can.

I'm spiraling towards my orgasm and he doesn't slow his pace. He keeps whacking against my pussy and my moans increase in loudness the closer I get to coming. When I chant, "Fuck me," he really lights into my pussy, and drills into me roughly.

When he pushes one of my knees towards my chest, the new angle tips me over the edge. "Oooooh, fuck!" I scream out, and he still doesn't stop fucking me. The orgasm lasts forever, and the room spins so much I have to close my eyes.

As I come down from my peak, I assume he's going to come soon as well, and I try to relax as tiny aftershocks of pleasure ripple through me.

"Do you," he pants between thrusts, "want to know… why your husband… chose me?"

Oooh, I do! "Yes," I groan as he rams me particularly hard. The zing of pleasure makes me wonder if I could come again.

He stops and removes his cock. Wait, what's going on?

"Get up on all fours."

Oooh, hell yes. I scramble onto my hands and knees, and he positions himself behind me. He grasps my hip with one hand and uses his other to guide his cock into my sopping wet hole. As he slides in, I sigh in delight. Him behind me is so fucking amazing.

Once he's inside, he slides his hands to my waist to make me grind against him as he jackhammers into me. Oh, fuck. I close my eyes again and clutch the comforter, trying to help stabilize myself.

"He chose me… because… I take a really long time… to come."

Ohhh, damn. Love for my husband floods through me, and I come all over Owen's cock a second time. He fucks me furiously and I cry out nonsense as the rapture ripples from my head to my toes. My second orgasm doesn't slow him down and he jackhammers into my pussy, giving me the roughest fuck of my life. The pleasure mounts again and I realize I'm going to come a third time right before I tip over the edge again.

"Ooooh, fuck," I scream out. The orgasm is so intense, I lower my forehead to rest against my arms as my entire body trembles from the force of my climax.

I'm not sure how long Owen continues to fuck me, but at some point I come again. Afterwards he slows his thrusts down until he's stroking slowly. My brain is so fuzzy, and the pleasure is so intense, I'm almost surprised when he finally comes with a roar. My pussy is a quivering mess and I milk his cock, making sure he's unloaded all his cum before he pulls out.

As soon as he moves away from my ass, I collapse onto my stomach and he stretches out next to me.

"Fuck, that felt good," he pants. "Thank you, Jessica."

I mumble, "Thank you too," as my pussy throbs. I might just fall asleep right here.

The bed jostles as he gets up and I faintly hear him get dressed. I'm floating in a wonderful daze when Lucas comes in. The guys talk briefly, and Owen thanks him for a great night. They both leave the room and my eyes are closed when Lucas returns. He spreads my legs, and I try to help him but I'm out of energy.

This is the part of the night I look forward to the most. After I fuck another guy, Lucas is desperate to have me and his need to fill me with his cum is the best thing ever. I sigh in ecstasy as Lucas enters me tenderly and rests on top of me, pressing me into the bed. He makes love to me softly and the gentle waves of pleasure wash over me.

When I come again, I can only give a soft moan as stars explode behind my eyes. I'm dazed and spinning when Lucas comes with a loud groan. As his hot cum paints my cave walls, my entire body glows with love for him. I can tell Ms. Kitty is going to be sore tomorrow, and I smile as I feel the deep ache.

Lucas promised me a hard pounding, and damn, he sure delivered.

The End

Shared Hotwife at the Con

Chapter 1

I'm hyper-focused on my monitor as I type away at a werewolf breeding erotic romance, so I don't notice my husband, Lucas, walk into our home office until he drops a manila envelope in front of me. Pressing my lips together, I hold in my annoyance at having something tossed at me while I'm in the middle of the important breeding scene where the woman is about to get knotted by three shifters. I've been so busy today I didn't even take the time to get dressed after my shower and just threw on a nightgown and called it good. I tug at the neckline and roll my shoulders to loosen the muscles as I pick up the envelope and turn it over. There's no writing on either side.

"What's this?"

He shrugs casually but I can tell he's suppressing a grin, so whatever's in the envelope must be exciting to him.

"That, my wonderful wife, is our travel itinerary for a trip we're taking next month."

Whoa, Lucas planned a trip to surprise me? Has he ever done that? It's like Christmas and my birthday all wrapped up in one. About twice a year, I spend a long weekend at a luxury spa resort. He never goes with me, and I prefer it that way since it's the time I focus on myself, but I'd hinted last week that I'd like to take more vacations with him.

I hadn't expected him to take action so quickly and a surge of adrenaline makes my hands shake as I open the envelope and pull out a stack of printouts. Two tickets fall in my lap and I pick them up and study them. They're for a comic con in San Diego, California next month. Um, when

I asked for a vacation I pictured sandy beaches or an adult lifestyle resort. Attending comic cons isn't really my thing.

Flipping through the printed-out papers confirms it's all related to the upcoming trip: hotel, flight information, and details about the con. Shit, I guess I'm going to a con. I try sounding enthusiastic and I study the hotel information. At least it looks like a nice hotel.

"So, we're going to California. Is something fantastic happening at the con?"

He laughs, as if I made a joke. "We've been talking about going for years, and I decided to surprise you. You wanted to take more vacations."

Oh shit, he has been talking about going to one, but I didn't know it included travel. We live in Oregon, close to Portland, so there has to be a local one, right? I was noncommittal every time he talked about it since I didn't want to kill his dreams, but I assumed it would be a day trip and not a big deal. The passes to the con are for all four days. Five nights plus a few hours on a plane is a big deal. Yeah, that's so not in my plans.

He moves behind me and massages my shoulders while I scan the papers. I don't know how to respond.

"Baby, the best thing is that I pre-planned this with Miri. She's been keeping your schedule clear for the trip."

Miri has been my best friend since middle school, and she's also my personal assistant who handles pretty much everything to do with my indie publishing except the actual writing. I didn't even question why she was giving me specific deadlines and telling me when things needed to be done. But now it's obvious she was ensuring I'd be finished with my book and not stressing about the trip.

I'm not sure whether to murder her for not giving me the heads-up that Lucas was planning this, or thank her for keeping my blissful ignorance going as long as she could. Lucas is thrilled and expecting me to jump for joy, but I'm still in shock and I'm not sure how I want to react.

"And Jessica, I was thinking... It's been a while since our trip to the Temptations Resort. If someone caught your eye in San Diego, we could have a little fun."

A shiver of longing runs through me straight to Ms. Kitty — the pet name for my pussy — and she wakes up. A kick of desire reminds me of what happened when we went to Temptations. It's a lifestyle resort, and there were plenty of men to play with. Ms. Kitty got quite the workout.

Lucas's hands continue to work the knots out of my neck and shoulders, and I groan. He's always been marvelous with his hands. The offer of playing with someone while in San Diego, plus the neck massage, melts any further resistance. Since he misinterpreted what type of vacation I wanted, I better have him spell out what his offer on the trip includes.

"So what exactly are you thinking when you say 'have some fun'?"

He runs his hands down my spine and tugs on my pajamas until I lean forward so he can slip his hands underneath the nightshirt. He skims along my skin as he moves the fabric up towards my shoulder and a tremor of awareness runs through me from the brush of his fingers.

"Put your hands in the air."

Oh, okay. I'm not totally sure where this is going, but I'm liking the direction. I lift my hands towards the ceiling and he pulls my nightshirt off over my head, leaving me with only my panties on. Since I wasn't planning on leaving the house today, I'm not wearing a bra. My nipples pucker, partly from the cold air and partly from dirty thoughts of what he might do to me. I could sit on the edge of the desk while he hammered away and whispered filthy things in my ear. Mmm, yeah...

He swivels my office chair to face him and he drops to his knees, spreading my legs so he can kneel between them. A low pleasant hum warms my blood. I'm good with him on his knees. He cups my breasts and I moan as he rubs my nipples between his index fingers and thumbs.

"My idea..." He pauses and leans forward to lick a nipple, and I draw in my breath as a spike of bliss swirls in my core.

He continues, "I'm thinking that I would check the app for a guy who you could play with one night. Does that sound good?"

He draws one of my nipples between his lips and sucks on it while I moan and run my fingers through his hair.

"Yeah, I could be agreeable to that."

Oh, fuck yeah. The best thing about being married to Lucas is that not only do I get tons of sex with him whenever we go on vacation, but he also gets horny whenever other guys check me out. It always ends up with some other guy's cock inside me while Lucas listens through a wall and strokes himself.

It's easy to find guys on vacation willing to fuck a hotwife, and it helps that I'm petite with large breasts and naturally blonde hair. I've always attracted attention based on my looks, and I find it amusing that the attention is increasing as I age. At 33, I have tons more guys drooling over me than when I was in my early 20s and in college.

When I was younger, I underestimated the allure of a woman who knows what she wants and has sexual experience. I assumed that by the time I was married and in my 30s, I'd be settled into a boring life and men would spend their time ogling younger women. But nope, the dating pool is actually larger now because younger men and older men both eye me. Yeah, this is an awesome age.

Lucas pushes against my shoulder, tips the office chair back, and hooks his hands around my knees to pull me closer to him and the edge of the chair. He kisses down my stomach and spreads my legs further apart. My blue panties are basic cotton and nothing special, and they already have a small wet patch. I'll let him think it was all him and had nothing to do with the sexy scene I was writing. He fingers my pussy through the fabric and desire swirls in my core.

When he hooks his fingers into the sides of my panties, I lift my ass off the chair so that he can pull them down. He spreads my legs wider and gives Ms. Kitty little kisses. He uses his thumbs to spread apart my nether lips, and I moan in anticipation.

"Oh god," I whimper as his tongue snakes out and slips inside me.

My hips buck up for more and he moves his mouth to my clit to suck and lick my swollen bean. This is heaven. If he keeps doing this, I'll agree to anything he wants.

"Mmmm, yes. Like that."

Lucas is fabulous at oral, and after so many years with me, he knows exactly how to make me come fast. When he sticks his tongue into my pussy as far as he can, I spasm around it and moan like a greedy slut while.

Grabbing fistfuls of his hair, I press his face further into my center and he moves his mouth back up to my clit to give it more attention. My vision is fuzzy from ecstasy when I peek down at him. His eyes glow hotly as he locks his gaze with mine and presses his fingers into my exposed wetness. I let go of his hair and squirm against his fingers.

"Tell me why you love me." I whisper.

He lowers his eyes to examine my wide-open legs. The heat in my core rises another degree as he stares at a wet Ms. Kitty. He's the only man I feel this free with, and the intimacy of the moment makes my breath hitch.

"You're my everything. I've never loved anyone but you. Not even close."

I moan at his words as my eyes drift shut, and he leans forward and licks my sensitive clit as he slides his fingers in and out of me. He continues to finger fuck me slowly, and when he makes a hook with his finger to massage my cave wall, I shudder uncontrollably at the impending climax.

He can tell I'm close, so he pumps faster and harder. When the orgasm hits, I scream as my body vibrates with euphoria.

"Ohhhh, god!"

I clench around his fingers as I ride out the waves of bliss, lost in mindless pleasure. When I come down from the peak, I drop back into the chair and sigh while Lucas strokes his hand against my pussy.

"You're still soaking. Just how I like you."

He kisses my thigh, and I open my eyes and glance lovingly at him. When he grins, his face shines with my juices and his eyes twinkle wickedly.

He announces, "My turn now," and stands, holding out his hand to me. "Baby, we're not done yet."

Ohhh, maybe I'll get another orgasm. I clasp his hand and he helps me up. Once I've found my balance, I step towards the door, expecting to go to the bedroom, but he stops me.

"No, baby. I want you to bend over your desk."

Pleasure pulses in my veins as I put my elbows on the surface of my desk and wiggle my ass at him. He steps up behind me and caresses an ass cheek while I give him a low hum of appreciation in the back of my throat. He's wearing sweatpants, and it only takes him a few seconds to pull out his cock and rub it up and down my slick folds.

Even though I already had an orgasm, I'm desperate for that first thrust. I sway my hips, trying to entice him.

"Mmm, that feels so good. I need you inside me."

He taps his cock against me, not pushing it in.

"Ask me to fuck you."

My head spins as I grip the edge of my desk and shimmy my hips, massaging the tip of his cock with my velvety wetness. My body is on fire, and I tense up for the first plunge.

"Oh god, please fuck me."

He removes his cock and I mewl in displeasure. What is he doing? A sharp smack on my ass makes me cry out.

"Shit! Please?"

He grabs my hips and gives a sexy growl.

"Yes, I think I will."

With one lunge, Lucas drives straight to my core and I have to stand on my tiptoes as he shoves me forward against the desk.

"Fuuuck!"

He immediately bulldozes into my pussy, clearly not intending to make me come again unless I can do it fast. Whenever he fucks me like this, it's as if I'm a toy and only here for his amusement. It hits a filthy kink of mine, and my brain short circuits as he uses me. This isn't my gentle, loving husband. This is the rough side that occasionally comes out, and I love it.

He knocks against me and each thrust causes ripples of pleasure to wash over me. I'm moaning and panting as he holds onto my hips and fucks me vigorously. The chorus of our moans fill the air, and every time he bottoms out, his balls whack against my clit and create a wet slap. All I can do is grip the edge of the desk for leverage and hold on as he rides me.

Oh, holy fuck. I'm dizzy from the rapture, and I hear myself chanting for him to fuck me harder. He groans as he speeds up.

"Do you like this, baby?"

My muscles tighten, and I'm half out of my mind from the continuous assault of delight.

"Yes. God... Yes!"

He slams into me with a fury and I give in to my orgasm when he hits a pleasurable spot repeatedly. I scream as my second white-hot climax rips through me. He fucks me through my orgasm, and as my cave walls shudder and milk his cock, he comes with a grunt and fills me. His warm stickiness coats me as he pistons in and out, pumping every last drop into me.

When he finally slows down and pulls out, I'm relaxing on my desk, fuzzy and floating in a warm place. I could fall asleep right here, but Lucas doesn't let me. I give a tiny protest as he helps me stand up. Ugh, I don't want to move. He holds me steady while I get my bearings.

When the lust fog clears, I understand he's taking care of me and can't leave me on the desk. I probably don't really want to sleep right there, but it felt nice for a moment.

I murmur, "Thanks," and blow him a kiss.

Since I don't plan on putting my nightshirt back on, I use it to wipe some of our joint wetness off his cock before he adjusts himself back into his sweatpants. His cum drips down the inside of my thighs, and I don't bother cleaning it up. This mess is going to require a shower, but I don't care about that now. I'll nab some clean clothes and take a shower before bed.

I slide my hand into his. "Come on, Lucas, let's find food and talk about the trip."

After that good of a fucking, he gets whatever he wants. He'll never know I didn't want to go on the trip. Besides, he promised me a playdate.

Chapter 2

The luxury hotel where Lucas reserved a room isn't far from the convention center and we check in the night before the con starts. Even though the flight to San Diego wasn't long, we're both tired from working part of the week and from the added stress of travel, so we crash early.

Since this comic con is for Lucas, I decided to skip the first day and looked up what amenities the hotel spa offered and booked a package for the works. I'm going to stay at the hotel and he's going to meet up with a couple of guys he knows for the gaming night after the opening ceremonies.

This is the first break from writing I've taken in months and I need to unwind. He thinks it's crazy that I'd prefer to spend the day at the spa than watching the gaming tournaments, but the spa is what I need to stay sane. Whenever I take my long weekends at a wellness spa, I get pampered and come home feeling like a new woman. I'm hoping one day at the spa here has the same effect.

He worries over me while we get dressed. "Will you be okay by yourself all day? I don't know when I'll be back."

I laugh. "Yes, hon. I'm looking forward to relaxing."

Knowing he doesn't want to ditch me fills me with warmth, but this is what I adore about being married to him. We both can enjoy separate activities without being joined at the hip.

After a late breakfast, I kiss Lucas goodbye and take the elevator down to the lobby for my spa day. I have back-to-back appointments and I spend several hours getting a massage, a facial, and a mani-pedi. Ms. Kitty gets professionally groomed as well. She needs to be a pretty kitty if we find a playmate.

Dinner is takeout from a local sushi bar, and since I'm not expecting Lucas back for hours, I put on a silk nightgown and relax on the couch to stream the latest Thor movie — Love and Thunder — while I eat my yummy dinner. I need to watch Thor for inspiration to get in the mood for the con tomorrow. It's research... I swear.

A month ago, Lucas invited a guy to the house to fuck me and the guy reminded me of Loki. Ever since then, it's been a running joke that I'm going to fuck a Thor lookalike on this trip. When the movie finishes, I lie on the couch and daydream about a hunky guy plowing me against the wall just out of eyesight from everyone at the con. Will there even be a quiet corner to fuck someone?

Lucas should get back to the hotel so I can ride him and imagine he's my own Thor. Ms. Kitty buzzes with approval and I move a hand to fondle her through my panties. My phone beeps with a text from Lucas, and I stop rubbing myself to check the message.

Lucas: I'm getting some beers with friends. Are you OK?

Me: Yep, have fun. Don't do anything I *would* do.

I end the message with a kissy face emoji, and I sigh as I set my phone on the coffee table. Well, shit. No sexy husband to ride. He's usually no good to me after a few hours drinking with his friends. Ms. Kitty complains that I'm ignoring her, and I slide my hand underneath my panties and head straight for my clit. I sigh with yearning as I caress lazy circles around my bundle of nerves. I'm not sure if I plan on going for the big O yet, or If I'm going to just give myself a pleasant edge.

My phone beeps again, and this time Lucas sends me a picture of a couple laughing at the bar. They're posed towards the camera, so I can tell Lucas didn't take the picture on the sly. Both are cosplaying and the woman looks like the cute brunette with the glasses from the Thor movie, and the guy with her looks like Thor did at the beginning of the movie in jeans, t-shirt, and a sleeveless red leather jacket. The picture includes a message.

Lucas: I found your Thor.

My entire body lights up and a shock of delight ripples down my spine. Wait, there's no way that guy is for me. Plus, he has a woman with him.

The way the guy's arm is around the woman in the picture says they're together. I laugh at how quickly I flushed. Lucas enjoys teasing me when he sees guys he knows I'd have fun fucking. I message Lucas back.

Me: That's not nice. Ms. Kitty thought you were serious for a moment and now she's angry at you.

Lucas: I'm almost sorry.

Me: You can make it up to us tomorrow. I'm going to bed. I'll probably be asleep when your tipsy ass gets back here.

Lucas: Okay, baby. I'll see you soon. Love you.

Me: Love you.

Hmm, do I want to go to bed or should I keep touching myself and get really horny? I slip my hand back into my panties and caress my clit... as if I really was going to do anything else. That's crazy talk.

My thoughts turn dark and naughty as I imagine a muscular guy sliding inside me. Yeah, that's what I need. My toes curl as I spread my legs wider and use my other hand to finger fuck myself. The desire to orgasm hits me and I moan loudly. Yeah, okay, there's no stopping this.

I rub my clit faster and continue to daydream about a long-haired hunk spearing into me relentlessly. It doesn't take long until I'm close to coming. When I push another digit into my pussy, the added thickness shoots me over the edge. I cry out as pleasure radiates from my core, but the orgasm is shorter than I want. I come down quickly and the euphoria dies off.

My fingers didn't do the job as well as Lucas's cock would have. Should I try for another one? A big yawn breaks my train of thought. Yeah, maybe not. The hotel claims it has top-of-the-line mattresses, and the one in my room is calling to me.

Wiping my hands on my panties, I drag myself off the couch and get ready for bed. I'm sound asleep by the time Lucas gets back and I stir only slightly when he gets into bed.

"Love you, hun," I murmur.

He kisses my shoulder. "I love you too, baby."

I'm asleep again before he turns off the bedside lamp.

The next morning, I'm examining myself in the bedroom mirror while I wait for Lucas to be ready to leave the hotel. I didn't really want to cosplay, and I just wanted to wear the sexiest black leather outfit I own. But when I told Lucas the plan, he was adamant that I needed to bring fishnet stockings so I could be Black Canary. I can't argue with the results. I'm sexy as all fuck in black leather and fishnets.

When Lucas leaves the bathroom, he's dressed like Green Arrow and I give an appreciative whistle. Neither of our costumes are super authentic, but at least we're trying. Plus, I can spend all day imagining what my roleplaying Green Arrow hubby is going to do to me tonight. He promised to make things up to me today and we've been too busy this morning.

He gives me a kiss on the cheek. "Are you ready to go?"

I double check I put everything we need in my black backpack and slide it over my shoulders. I have to get on my tiptoes to give him a peck, and I bounce on the heels of my combat boots.

"Yep, let's do this."

Lucas orders us a ride-share car and as we leave the hotel, several people in the lobby glance in our direction. I overhear a kid asking his mother if we're superheroes. I don't hear her response, but I hope she said yes. Lucas told me that Black Canary's superpower is the canary cry where her scream creates ultrasonic vibrations that can hurt people and break objects. She's also good in hand-to-hand combat, an expert motorcyclist, and a covert operative and investigator. I straighten my five-foot nothing frame and swagger to give the illusion of confidence. I'm cosplaying as a badass, and I might be small, but I'm mighty.

It takes a while to get to the convention center due to traffic and the sheer horde of cosplayers swarming the streets. The line to get our badges is crazy long, but they keep us moving at a steady pace. While we're waiting, Lucas tells me about a fight that broke out yesterday at the con that included yelling and someone punching another guy. I hope everyone is okay, but with this many people in one location, I'm not surprised that tempers would flare. I'm already cranky at all the people who are standing in the middle of the hallways.

We're soon through the line and join the main crush of people moving through the convention center. The best thing about the con is all the awesome cosplaying, and it's fun to look at everyone. The creativity of the costumes pings the writing side of my brain and I've already got several storylines brewing in the back of my head. I'll need a new pen name if I did anything but paranormal romance, but who knows, maybe it's time to branch out. Horny Hotwife at the Con has a nice ring to it.

Cell reception is spotty, so I decide to stick with Lucas so I don't have to find him later. I've been turned on all morning and I see several handsome men that I wouldn't mind riding, but there's so much to do that I'm distracted from my horniness. The plan is to find a souvenir for Miri and something cute and cuddly for myself — If it has glitter on it, even better. I'm not really sure what I want, but I figure I'll know it when I see it. The artwork distracts me. Some of it is amazing, and I'd love to support other indie artists. I tug on Lucas's hand.

"Hey, where's the sales floor? I have a backpack that needs filling."

Lucas laughs and he starts telling me something about a panel he wants to attend that starts soon, but as he talks, a guy who looks like Thor catches my eye. I'm preoccupied and I don't hear the rest of what Lucas says. Wait, is that the same guy who was in his picture last night? If it is, today he's wearing full battle armor and carrying a fake Stormbreaker weapon. Ms. Kitty hums to life as I study him. He's muscular and just all-over massive. I daydream about kneeling in front of him and sucking on his cock. I'd like to see how many licks it takes to get to the center of that lollipop.

"Earth to Jessica."

Lucas waves his hand in front of my face, and I give him a huge grin.

"Uh... See that dude over there by the wall?" I gesture towards Thor. "Is that the guy from the bar?"

Lucas's eyes follow my hand. "Oh hey. Yeah, that's James."

Now that I've seen James in the flesh, I am so down with the idea of his cock inside me, but wouldn't Lucas have made plans if James was single and interested? I try to act casual, as if I'm not desperate for the guy's cock.

"Was the woman in the picture his girlfriend? She's not with him right now."

"Nah, she's dating another guy. I'm not sure how those two know each other, but she was making out with the other guy later."

I peer at James with even more interest. Why didn't Lucas hook me up with him? You'd think with how we've been joking for weeks about finding me a Thor, he would have made it happen.

"If you're done drooling over James, we need to get in line."

Ugh, fine. Lucas takes my hand and I prepare to wait. I know this is the main thing he's here for, but I'd rather check out the eye candy and shop.

While we wait in line, Lucas chats with people about our costume and where we're from. I spend the time trying not to stare at any one person for too long, and daydreaming plots for stories I will probably never write. The longer it takes, the more X-rated my stories become. Shit, we should have gotten up early and fucked like rabbits so I didn't spend the day horny looking at hot guys in costumes.

I catch a few of the guys checking me out and I see appreciation in their eyes at how I'm dressed, but everyone is polite and no one is leering or making me uncomfortable. We're eventually let into a large conference room with rows of chairs, but I'm more interested in crowd watching than anything else. Some costumes are incredibly elaborate, and there are more than a few people strolling around in shoes that are going to kill their feet within an hour. I'm thankful for my combat boots, since it seems like today is going to be a lot of standing around.

Right before the lights dim, I spot James across the room. God, he's so yummy. If I could get him alone, he's the type of guy I would totally fuck in a bathroom. I recently hooked up with a dude in a haunted house, so the bathroom at a con seems tame compared to what filthy things I did on Halloween.

I catch Lucas's eye, and he nods towards James.

"Are you going to spend all day imagining fucking James?"

"Hey, it's not my fault that we haven't had sex on the trip. You're the one who got drunk last night and left me all alone in the hotel with nothing else to do but touch myself and think about getting railed by a sexy, muscular guy."

I hadn't told him what I had done last night, and he perks up when I say I was touching myself.

He thinks for a second. "I don't know. I'm feeling a lack of appreciation for the hard work I put in last night."

The tone of his voice tells me he's teasing.

"Yeah, I'm sure laughing and drinking with your friends was oh so hard."

Lucas leans over, kisses below my ear, and whispers, "Yeah, but baby, I was also arranging for James to come to the hotel room tonight and fuck you."

Lust zips through my body, and my nipples harden as my pussy buzzes. I gape at Lucas.

"Really?"

I can't keep the excitement out of my voice, and I want to squeal and bounce. Jesus Christ, I really have married the most amazing man ever.

"Yes, really. But you have to pay attention to me today if you want to play with James tonight."

Oh hell yeah, I'll give Lucas so much attention, he'll be begging me to fuck James later just to get a break. I turn towards him, giving him my full attention and I take his hand, squeezing it.

"Okay, my love. I only have eyes for you today."

He laughs and his, "Uh-huh," tells me he doesn't fully believe me. So yeah, I might glance at other people, but Ms. Kitty and I are only interested in two people tonight. I want a hard pounding from James, and then I want my incredible husband to fuck me and tell me he loves me.

Chapter 3

Once Lucas tells me I'll be fucking the Thor lookalike tonight, I'm in a sexual daze and unable to concentrate on much. It doesn't help that Lucas is using every opportunity to fondle my ass, or standing close behind me when we're at a vendor booth so he can brush against me. I try pushing my ass back to get more contact, but all I'm doing is making myself hornier. By late afternoon I'm ready to shove Lucas against a wall and have my way with him in front of everyone. God, he's such a tease.

I saw James several times throughout the day. It's a big convention, but he seemed to orbit the same areas we were in. It's possible he's just so damn sexy and a massive guy so he stands out above the crowd. One time he was posing for pictures and holding Stormbreaker in a battle pose. He should have gone with a previous version of Thor so he'd have his hammer, Mjöllnir. He missed a genuine opportunity with that one, because now how can anyone joke about him hammering them, or wanting to touch his massive hammer? And what is Stormbreaker anyway? A battle axe? I don't even know, since I may have possibly been paying too close attention to the eye candy in the movie last night. I'm surprised I remember the names.

I take plenty of pictures to show Miri, always asking permission first, but most people seem to enjoy being photographed in their costumes. One of my favorites is a woman in a cow print bikini with a bell around her neck. The Wi-Fi sucks at the convention, so I can't send them to Miri immediately. I'll surprise her with them later. She'll love the cow bell.

Since I want to get Miri a souvenir for being wonderful and helping Lucas keep the trip a secret, we hunt the vendors for the perfect, funny, present. I spot a vendor selling high-end fantasy dildos. Oh yeah, Miri needs a dragon dildo... the biggest they sell. Dragging Lucas over to the vendor, I can see he's trying to pretend he's not interested until I start examining the enormous ones.

"Uh, Jessica?"

I'm busy trying to choose between a red or a blue one and give him a distracted, "Hmmm?"

"Is this for Miri or for you?"

I pause and blink at him. "Good point. I'll get both."

As I pay for the dildos and tuck them safely in my backpack, Lucas mutters, "I didn't mean you should buy them both."

I ignore him, lost in thought. Do I want to keep the red or the blue one for myself? Eh, I don't have to decide today. I'll figure it out when I get home.

Hooking my arm through his, I grin at him. "If you treat me nicely, I might let you use it on me."

He perks up and kisses my cheek. "Once you're screaming my name tonight, you'll beg me to stuff you with it."

Wet heat flares between my legs and anticipation flickers through me. Jesus, this afternoon can't end fast enough. A glance at my phone tells me I still have a couple of hours to go. Fuck.

By the time we get back to the hotel, I'm ready to shove Lucas on the bed, straddle him, and grind against his hardness. I'm not sure I even need James at this point. My husband's cock will do the trick within a few minutes.

Lucas sits on the bed and types a message on his phone while I unlace my boots and drop them to the floor with a loud thud. Tossing my leather jacket on the back of a chair, I quickly strip. Lucas doesn't know what's in store for him, but as soon as I'm naked, he's mine. As I peel the fishnets down my legs, Lucas distracts me.

"Hey, James will be here in 30 minutes. I'm going to go downstairs and get some snacks. Do you want to take a shower?"

Desire swirls in my stomach as my nipples harden. Well hell, I suppose I can wait 30 minutes.

"Yeah, I'll take a quick one."

I bring the sexy lingerie I plan to wear tonight into the bathroom with me and turn the shower on so the water can heat. What I really need is a good fuck. It's difficult to think of anything else. I wasn't always this randy, but once we started our hotwife arrangement, my sex drive easily doubled. Just thinking about Lucas fucking me after James is done with me gives me shivers and I press my thighs together. We both love this arrangement and I don't see us stopping.

Being a hotwife is awesome, and I didn't know how fulfilling it would be. I always assumed if you had an open marriage, both partners got to play with other people. I wouldn't have guessed there were men out there who wanted their wife to fuck other guys without them having equal opportunity with other women. Lucas says he's perfectly content with this arrangement and this is very much about my pleasure. What we do works for us because Lucas is in control of the situation. I'm not out fucking random men and we're very much doing this together, even if Lucas isn't in the room. It might be a weird relationship to some people, but we're happy.

My shower takes longer than I planned since I was ruminating. I'm dressed and almost ready, but I'm still in the bathroom when James knocks on our hotel door. All my senses ping alive and I feel myself growing wet, despite having just dried off. I hear the men's voices through the door, but I can't make out what they're saying.

After I blow dry my hair, I smooth my silk negligee over my stomach to quell the sudden butterflies fluttering around in there. With how turned on I am, there's no way this won't have a happy ending, so I shouldn't be nervous. As I step out of the bathroom, the men are telling jokes and laughing, and it eases some of my concerns.

The suite is one large room, and they're sitting on the couches along one wall. Oh damn, James isn't wearing his costume. It looked uncomfortable long-term, so I guess that's for the best. He's wearing jeans and a blue t-shirt with Captain America's shield on it. I almost laugh at that, but his bulging biceps sidetrack me. Oh, hell yes. He looks too big for the hotel couch. Please God, let him have a cock that matches his size.

"Jessica, this is James."

Oh, heh. I guess we haven't met, despite me fantasizing about him all day.

I smile and give him a soft, "Hi."

The twinkle in James's eye when he says, "Hi," in return does dangerous things to my inhibitions. He could bend me over any surface and have me begging within seconds. I didn't bother wearing underwear, and with how wet I am, his cock would slide right in.

Lucas rises from the couch and comes over to kiss me. As his lips claim mine, I wonder if this is for show. I'm assuming he's going to be in the bathroom listening, since there isn't any other door he can hide behind. He's stroking my tongue with his, and I'm mentally fuzzy when he stops.

"Baby, tonight is going to be different."

"Different, how?"

I'm addlebrained with lust, and I don't care what happens as long as I get fucked. Lucas's eyes are dark with desire while he caresses my cheek with his thumb.

"I'm going to sit on the couch and watch."

Whoa, what? A shiver of arousal heads straight for my clit and I almost moan at the thought of Lucas in the room. He's never watched before, and sometimes I wished he would. This is a delightful surprise.

"You're sure?" I ask, moving my hand between us and rubbing along the hardness in his trousers as I search his face. He's clearly turned on, and he groans, "Yes," as I fondle the length of him through the fabric. He presses against me for a moment and then steps back out of reach.

"Have fun, baby."

Lucas takes a spot on the couch in clear view of the bed and it hits me how different this is, knowing he's going to watch. I've been wanting to fuck James all day and now that the moment is here, I'm uncertain how to get the ball rolling because Lucas is in the room. I swing my arms and try to not look nervous.

My pulse quickens as James approaches me, and I realize how enormous he is compared to my petite frame. His thigh muscles strain the fabric of his jeans, and his narrow waist gives him a V shape since his shoulders are broad. I lick my lips as I focus again on the defined muscles in his arms... Mmm yeah, those arms.

He's going to have to make the first move, and I wait as he slides his arms around my waist, pulling me towards him. The clean scent of fresh pine clings to him, and I can tell he showered before coming. A forbidden longing burns in my core as he brushes his lips against mine. He's thorough, but tender, as if he's giving me time to say no. It helps ease the rest of my nervousness, and I'm able to enjoy the sensations he's creating within me. The need for his cock grows stronger every second.

When he deepens the kiss, his tongue tangles with mine — hot and playful — and I want more. My head whirls, and I moan as I throw myself into his embrace, almost forgetting Lucas is watching in my attempt to devour James's mouth.

James breaks off the kiss, and his voice is husky with need. "You smell nice, like coconuts."

I wasn't expecting him to notice my body wash, and I giggle. "Thank you, you smell good too."

James leans in and nibbles on my neck and my knees feel weak when he touches me this way.

His voice rumbles in my ear. "You're so beautiful."

I'm warm and tingling from his nearness. He's doing a fabulous job with seduction so far, and I run my fingers through his long, dirty-blonde hair. He takes hold of one of my wrists and moves my hand down to the hardness in his pants. Oh shit, this is hot. The wetness in my core increases and desire courses through me as his cock throbs against my hand. I can tell his cock is huge, and my pussy clenches and my breathing quickens as I wonder how much longer it'll be until he slides that monster inside me.

The noise of Lucas shifting on the couch makes me glance in his direction. He's still in his costume, and his cock is out of his pants. He's slowly stroking as he watches us. The soft smile on his face is all I need to see. My love for Lucas envelops me, and all my concerns about him being in the room fade. I'm ready to give Lucas the show of his life so he'll want to watch more often.

James rocks his hips, forcing me to smooth my palm over his hard length. He moans quietly as he bites at my earlobe. The inside of my thighs are slick with moisture and there isn't an ounce of patience left in me. I need him inside me right now, and I'm going to do whatever it takes to hurry this along.

Squeezing his cock, I apply pressure and yank on him.

"Fuck!" he groans. "That feels amazing."

A sense of power builds inside me. Maybe I should take control and be the badass I assumed Black Canary was... small, mighty, and in charge.

I release his cock and step back, purring, "James, why don't you take those clothes off and lie on the bed?"

He lifts one eyebrow, and I don't have time to wonder what that means because he pulls his shirt off over his head and his well-defined abs distract me. Oh, hello. Yes, I will lick those soon. Ms. Kitty buzzes in appreciation of the view as James quickly removes the rest of his clothes, dropping them into a pile on the floor.

Once he's naked, he approaches me and my breath catches when he lifts the bottom of my negligee and strips it off me without warning.

"Beautiful," he growls and cups my breasts, rolling the nipples under his thumbs.

My heart races and I want to squeeze my thighs together in eagerness. Wait, I'm the one in charge, right? He walks me backwards to the bed and when the mattress touches my calves, I accept I misjudged the situation. He's taking control. A thrill courses through me at the thought of Lucas watching this. I bet he'll enjoy seeing me manhandled. This is what he always imagined was happening, and now he's witnessing it.

James presses on my shoulder and I sit on the edge of the bed. He moves to the side, so I twist my body, realizing he's giving Lucas a clear view of the action. James's cock is thick and the veins stand out along his shaft. It's slightly curved upwards towards his stomach, and saliva gathers in my mouth as I imagine sucking on it. He's so big and my hands are small, so it might require both of them to encircle it. Previously, I might have questioned if he would fit inside me, but after being with several large men, I know better. He'll stretch me out gloriously, but he'll fit. God, I love that first thrust, and his cock is going to be one to remember.

When he grasps the base of his shaft and moves a hand to the back of my head, I part my lips eagerly. This better only be a tasty snack before the main course. I wrap my mouth around his fat cockhead and suck. Okay, I'm not sure he's going to fit in my mouth. I've had bigger guys than this, but I didn't give them a blowjob. Fuck it, let's try.

James doesn't force anything, and I relax my jaw and ease him further inside. He barely fits, and he slides into my throat all the way to the hilt before pulling out. My eyes dart to Lucas and he's focused on the cock at my lips, so I grip the base of James's shaft with both hands and caress it while swirling my tongue around the fat tip. The heat of his body against mine gives me a pleasurable tingle, and dampness pools between my legs.

"You're incredible."

His voice is low as he slides into my mouth and fucks it slowly, allowing me plenty of air between strokes. His hips move faster and his moans are music to my ears. The longer he fucks my mouth, the more dazed from lust I become. I feel myself sink into the slutty mindset I crave. This is one of the amazing benefits of what Lucas and I do. I'm able to fully let go and become a fucktoy for these men, getting gratification while also driving Lucas wild.

When James pulls his cock out of my mouth and steps back out of reach, I mewl in displeasure. Damn him, I wasn't done with my treat.

"Get up on the bed on all fours. I want to see how tight your pussy is."

Yes... that. I scramble up on the bed, positioning myself so that Lucas will get a side view of James fucking me. Lucas is still stroking himself slowly while watching us, so I know he's having fun. James grasps my hips and pulls me closer to the edge and I lower my head, presenting him with a wet invitation. He rubs his length along my slit, and I moan as ecstasy swirls in my core.

"Is this what you want?"

He pokes me with just the tip of his cock, and I cry out. "Yes, please fuck me!"

I expected him to make me beg more, so when he slams straight into me, I moan again, louder, as I grind against him from the unexpected spike of bliss. Fuck, he's huge. I'm filled beyond belief, and it's wonderful. My fingers claw at the comforter, trying to stabilize myself as he drills into me.

The sensation is overwhelming, and my mind fogs as his shaft massages my cave walls. The tip of his cock knocks against a sensitive place deep inside with every thrust and sends a jolt of pleasure through my body.

"So wet and tight," he grunts.

James's dirty talk taps into my desire to be used like a toy, and I welcome the mindless rapture as I arch my back. A low sound of passion escapes my throat as he drives himself deeper, hitting the magical spot over and over again. He's ramming against me so hard that the bed creaks and the headboard thumps the wall. I give a silent prayer that no one is in the room next to us, but I'm too far gone to really care. The sounds coming from James are erotic as hell, and my pussy squeezes around his cock as I grip handfuls of bedding beneath me and cling on for dear life. I'm reeling as I edge closer to my orgasm.

I'm almost in shock when he pulls out before either of us come.

I attempt to protest, but it's a mumbled, "Wha…"

"Get on your back."

I obey immediately, and peek over at Lucas to make sure he's enjoying himself. He's a rapt audience and his eyes are glued to the show while he plays with his cock. I blow a kiss towards Lucas and he smiles as James climbs onto the bed and parts my raised knees.

I turn my attention back to James, and he grazes his thick cock against my clit. I rotate my hips, hoping he'll push inside me. He examines me with hungry eyes, and there's an animalistic glint to them that makes me want to beg him to fuck me as hard as he wants. I want to see what he'd do if unleashed, but I'm not able to speak coherently and can only moan as he torments me. Fuuuuck, I'm going insane.

When he finally sinks into me, it's a torturous, slow grind. His thick shaft pushes in, Inch by Inch, until he bottoms out. I whimper in pleasure as he rocks his pelvis, fucking my tightness. My face contorts as the joy increases. I can't take much more of this. His thickness massages every nerve ending I have, and it's impossible to concentrate. I've lost all rational thought in the desire to come. The tension builds inside me and I moan in delight with his next powerful thrust.

"You look like you're about to explode."

James sounds amused. His words make me undulate against him, so close to the brink, but I can't come while he's fucking me slowly.

"Yes... God, yes. Fuck me harder.... faster. I need to come!"

He speeds up, slamming into me vigorously. I stop trying to hold on to the bedding, and I grip his shoulders while wrapping my legs around him. Each hard whack against my pussy shoots fiery sparks down my spine.

"Ohhhh, god. I'm going to come."

Hot waves build in my center and I cry out as I peak. Pure ecstasy rushes from my fingertips to my toes and I writhe against him as he hammers into my quivering pussy. I'm dizzy as he uses me for his fulfillment, and I close my eyes and thrash under him while he fucks me through my orgasm. He slides his hands under my ass so he can hold me steady while he pounds away repeatedly. The sensation of being fucked with such force keeps the ripples of bliss going and my orgasm seems like it's never going to end.

He stiffens and moans as he roars with satisfaction. I gaze at him and watch in amazement as his eyes roll into the back of his head from pleasure. His cock pulses as his hot seed floods into me, filling me completely. My body trembles uncontrollably, still shuddering from the intense climax, even after he pulls free from me. A tiny part of me wishes he hadn't pulled out because that means my time with him is ending, but Lucas still needs to fuck me.

I'm panting with satisfaction when he climbs off the bed. He disappears into the bathroom with his clothes and I melt into the mattress, savoring the relaxation from the incredible orgasm.

Lucas chuckles. "Don't get too comfortable on that bed."

I mumble, "Mmm hmm, I won't," and he laughs again.

I float in contentment while Lucas and James talk. Before James leaves, he thanks me for the fun and I stir awake enough to say goodbye to him. Lucas brings over a bottle of water and insists I take a sip. It perks me up and I stretch out on my side while he sits on the bed with me and plays with my hair. This is nice, but his cock is a hard bulge in his pants and I want him to get his pleasure.

"Baby, you ready for more?"

He's still stroking my hair, and I lean into his hand. His fierce facial expression says he's desperate to come and he won't be gentle. I'm probably going to be sore in the morning. But this is how it goes every time he shares me, and we both crave the connection of him fucking me after the other men.

I beam at him. "I'm ready."

Chapter 4

He removes his costume, taking the time to fold it carefully, and clambers onto the bed as I raise my knees and part them for him. He kneels and nestles his cock against my pussy, but doesn't press in. Instead he strokes his shaft along my wetness, taunting me and working me up again. My eyelids flutter closed as the bliss builds. He better not edge me tonight. I want to come again.

"Did you enjoy James fucking you?"

I keep my eyes closed and nod. "Mmm, yes. So good."

Desires swirls in my core as he rocks against me, still not pressing in, but the pressure against my clit is wonderful. He leans over me and brushes his lips on my cheek. When he moves to my mouth, he kisses me thoroughly, probing the depths with his tongue while my pussy buzzes and demands his cock. I caress his arms and shoulders, trying to reach what I can, as an inferno of need builds inside me. I know his body almost as well as my own, and his muscles twitch beneath my hands as I search out the sensitive spots along his neck and sides. The ache from Ms. Kitty reaches new heights when he props himself up on one arm and moves his free hand over my breast, playing with a nipple.

His voice is soft. "I'm going to fuck you hard enough to make you scream."

His whisper contrasts with the harsh words, and I groan.

"Yes."

He rises to his knees and hooks his arms around my thighs, pressing my thighs up towards my chest.

"Hang on, baby."

Oh, shit. I wasn't expecting him to bend me like a pretzel tonight. The position opens me and he fits the head of his cock against my slit. He gives me a few seconds to get ready for the invasion before he slams home.

"Shit!"

My breath catches as he pounds into me. He's not tender and romantic, and if anyone saw us, they wouldn't understand that every movement is filled with love. He drills into me, whacking against my tender flesh, letting me know that I'm his to use however he chooses. I cry out from the impact but it only adds fuel to his fire. He pummels my cunt mercilessly until I'm moaning continuously in pleasure. I want us to orgasm together, but I can't take much more of this without coming.

He grasps my thighs and grinds his cock inside me as we both thump against one another. Fuck, his cock feels incredible. Spikes of rapture radiate from my core. Our bodies collide repeatedly, and he's in a frenzy. My muscles tighten like a bowstring, and I expect to skyrocket over the edge at any second.

He pushes my knees further forward until they are close to my ears. He knows exactly how flexible I am, and I cross my ankles behind my head. I move a hand down to my clit and furiously flick my bean while he kneels and pounds into me. My pussy is a mess from James's cum and my previous orgasm, and Lucas fucks me so hard that a chorus of wet slapping sounds mingles with our panting and moans. This is wonderfully vulgar, even though there's nothing wrong with what we're doing. We both enjoy it.

"I'm going to fuck you raw," he growls as his balls slap against my ass and I sigh in delight.

"Yes... yes! Fucking yes!"

Whenever he shares me, he fucks me harder than he does other nights, especially if the guy has an enormous cock. The bed rocks back and forth with every swift bang, and my mind blanks from ecstasy. He grips my nipples between his fingers and pulls hard on them before slapping each breast. I yelp in surprise and almost come. Ohhhh, fuck. The pleasurable pain is intense, and when he smacks them again, I can't stop my orgasm.

Throwing my head back, I scream out his name and erupt. My body jerks violently from extreme bliss, and he pistons his hips so hard and fast my head spins from the onslaught of pleasure. I watch him through a haze of lust as he grinds his cock inside me. My moans become whimpers as he continues to use me.

"Who owns you?" he growls.

When I moan and don't answer, he spanks my ass.

"Hey!"

Ms. Kitty tries to sputter alive from the slap, but two mind-blowing orgasms might be enough for her tonight. Yeah, she's a pain slut, but we all have our limits.

"Tell me who owns you."

A sheen of sweat glistens on Lucas's chest and his pained expression says he's trying to not come.

I lock eyes with him. "You. You own me."

He stiffens and cries out, "Yes," as he explodes, burying himself balls-deep inside me. His cock throbs as he shudders and releases hot spurts of his cum. When he slows his thrusts, I unwind my legs from behind my head and he helps me lower them into a comfortable position as he pulls out. He climbs over me so he can stretch out on the bed.

He wraps me up in his arms, completely encasing me. I lean against his chest, needing the skin contact as we both come down from our high. When he chuckles, I tip my head up and he's smiling down at me with love shining in his eyes, but also possessiveness. Mmm, yeah, this is one of the great things about being a hotwife. Lucas gets territorial after someone fucks me good, and I enjoy the attention for a few days as he doesn't like to be apart from me for very long.

He rubs circles on my back as our heart rates slow down. The utter relaxation makes me feel boneless and I want to just stay in bed and not move, but I'm going to need a shower before bed. Knowing Lucas he'll take a shower with me to soap me up, paying special attention to my tender bits. This is part of his aftercare when I've been ridden hard, and it's another reason I know I married the perfect guy for me.

He kisses my forehead and his voice rumbles through his chest.

"Are you glad you came on the trip?"

Wait, does he know I didn't really want to go? I try to keep my voice light.

"Hey, who said I didn't want to?"

He laughs softly. "Jessica, after all these years, you think I couldn't tell?"

I snuggle closer and nuzzle his neck. Okay, so maybe he's not clueless after all.

"Mmm, well, it's been a lovely trip so far. Who do you plan for me to fuck tomorrow?"

His bark of laughter is louder this time. "Oh no, you need a few more days to be reminded you're mine."

"What? Dammit, I thought you were going to find me a cosplaying Star Lord next."

He tilts my chin towards him and kisses me passionately.

"No, baby. Not this time. That's how I'm getting you to attend the next comic con."

A tingle runs through me at his words. Well, shit... I guess I'm going to become a fan of attending comic cons now.

The End

Sharing His Gift Twice

Chapter 1

After submitting my latest reverse harem vampire manuscript, I needed a break, at least a week of relaxation, with no deadlines, no nagging editors, nothing that wasn't about me. My initial plan was to treat myself to my favorite wellness spa for a start, but it was fully booked for Valentine's Day. Figures. Instead, I've been nude sunbathing in my backyard. The warmth on my skin is a balm to my senses, and I feel my creative energy recharging.

I'm content and drowsy as Lucas returns from work, striding onto the deck. The grogginess fades as my pulse quickens with anticipation. Yay, he's home. His voice rings out clearly.

"Hi baby. You're a sexy sight to come home to."

I squint against the bright sun and stare at him, feeling my cheeks flush as his words linger in the air. Ms. Kitty buzzes from his appreciative smile.

Yes, yes, I know. It may be silly, but I call my shaved pussy Ms. Kitty. She's been responsible for enough of my wildest misadventures. I figure she's earned her own name. Of course, it comes in handy to blame her when we're late to something because I seduced Lucas into bed. "No, it's not my fault, it was all Ms. Kitty. I swear!"

Our acquaintances think we have a demanding cat. Our close friends? They just smile.

Lucas is dressed in his typical work clothes: slacks and a button-down dress shirt. He undoes the cuffs of his sleeves. My stomach gives a soft growl from hunger, reminding me I forgot lunch. We always end up in bed on Valentine's Day, whether early or late, but I need food before he fucks me.

I question him. "Did you bring dinner home with you?"

He stops in his tracks, surprised. "Uh, no… I didn't know I was supposed to."

Oh, this man. Amirite? I mean, a smart husband would have thought about bringing home food on Valentine's Day, but we've been busy and time creeped up on us. I didn't even know it was Valentine's until this morning and I saw the date on my phone. The days blur together when you work from home.

A small part of me is hurt that he's treating this like any normal day. Just because I forgot doesn't mean it's okay for him to forget as well. But I'm determined to not spoil the night.

I want my Valentine's Day sex, dammit.

"Oh, I didn't say anything." I roll onto my side and prop myself up on an elbow. I want to drive him crazy, so without taking my eyes from his, I run my fingertips along the curves of my hip and stomach, lightly grazing the skin with soft swirls. My fingertips linger on my hip, and I give him my best sultry voice. "You were supposed to read my mind. I'm on vacation, remember? People on vacation don't cook."

He says nothing, but I can feel his eyes on me, burning with desire. I didn't *exactly* plan to be naked when he got home, but I know how to make the most of a situation. I've played this game for years now.

Rising from the lounge chair, I let my long, blonde hair cascade down my back before standing and stretching languidly. He doesn't reply, but he's staring at me with a lusty gaze. Despite only being five feet tall without heels, I've been blessed with curves in all the right places, especially my chest. My breasts are my not-so-secret weapon when it comes to Lucas. If I can't get him to make an order for delivery within minutes, then I'll be surprised. Very surprised.

I seductively blow him a kiss. "Don't you worry, I'll take care of it. Ms. Kitty had her heart set on teriyaki chicken, but I'm sure she'll love something else. She'll get over the disappointment eventually… probably tomorrow."

He yanks out his phone, his fingers already heading to the familiar app. "Does Ms. Kitty want the usual?"

I grin wickedly, inching closer to him. "Yes, order her favorite. I'm going to get dressed."

I brush my lips softly against his before spinning away. He usually makes me work harder than this to get what I want. He must be in a good mood.

❖

I slip into a pair of form-fitting cotton shorts and a tank top that hugs my breasts. My bare feet glide across the tile as I enter the kitchen to find Lucas pouring me a glass of white wine. I take the crystal glass from him and our fingers brush for a few seconds.

When I perch on a bar stool, our eyes meet in a knowing glance. Lucas smiles, a hint of mischief playing on his lips. We don't have wine with dinner every night. I want to joke with him he doesn't need me drunk to get me into bed tonight; I'm as close to a sure thing as he'll ever get. He probably wants to make tonight seem special since it's Valentine's Day and he obviously forgot.

I giggle at him. "You know what I like. Teriyaki and wine."

He winks at me before draining his first glass and promptly refilling it. Hey, he better slow down or else he won't be any good for me later. I'm about to say something, but he distracts me.

"Baby, today is extra special."

Yeah, no shit, it's Valentine's Day. I keep my thoughts to myself and I give him my best flirty smile.

"Every Valentine's Day is special."

He chuckles. "That's not the only reason. I also took the next two days off work."

"Oh?"

What's this? I perk up, and Ms. Kitty throbs with delight. I love it when he has days off and I don't need to be writing. Maybe we won't even get out of bed for two days. We can order food and alternate watching movies and fucking like rabbits. It will be an extended Valentine's Day celebration.

Lucas sets his glass on the counter. "I've been thinking about taking some time off. It's been a stressful year. I deserve to relax."

I nod. He does. He's an actuary, and he makes good money, but most nights he complains about feeling mentally drained when he gets home from work. Two whole days in bed with me should refresh him. I'll send him back to work with a shit-eating grin plastered on his face. I'll call it pussy relaxation therapy.

Wait, I guess I better make sure he doesn't have any grand plans before I chain him to the bed. "What are you going to do with your time off?"

"That depends on you." He moves around the counter, and I slowly turn on the chair to face him. My open legs are an invitation and Lucas stands between them. He towers over me, and I can feel the heat radiating from his body. He leans down and takes my chin in his hand, brushing his lips against mine and whispers, "I met someone at the gym. I want you to fuck him."

His voice sends a shiver down my spine. Now this is interesting. I pull back to see his facial expressions. "Who is it?"

He twirls some of my hair around his finger and plays with the silky strands. "His name is Brian."

It's rare for him to pick up someone he meets. Usually he finds guys who want to fuck me on some online forum. I like to joke it's a rent-a-bull website. No money is exchanged; these guys all agree to fuck me after Lucas shares a picture with them.

"And what, dear husband, makes Brian someone you think I'd want to fuck?"

This is the game we play. I try to sound uninterested, while Ms. Kitty does hula hoops at the thought of being stuffed by a stranger. Usually the guy has something special about him that makes Lucas choose him: a huge package, tons of stamina, great at licking pussy, something.

He kisses me again and licks his way up my neck. "Brian is hot, has a nice cock, and is super friendly. I met him in the gym locker room the other day and we started talking. I bragged about you and showed him a picture."

I interrupt him. "Which picture?"

His gaze glows with desire. "The one of you wearing the sexy Halloween bunny costume."

Oh yeah, that's a good one. "He liked the pic?"

Yeah, I'm totally fishing for compliments.

"He adored it, and then I told him about what happened in the haunted house."

My eyebrows rise while my body flushes from desire. "You told a stranger at the gym that I fucked a dude in a haunted house?"

God, I'm so aroused. I love it when he tells people how slutty I am.

He nods. "Yeah. He thought it was great and told me I'm lucky to have such an adventurous wife."

I take a sip of my wine. Uh-huh, he *is* lucky, but so am I. I'm damn grateful to have a husband who enjoys sharing me with other men without wanting to fuck around himself.

He takes another sip of his wine. "Anyway, after I told Brian about what happened at the comic con—"

I cut in again with a laugh. "Oh god, you told him I was a slut at the con also?"

My panties grow damp, knowing Lucas is spreading it around I'm a filthy whore and willing to open my legs for anyone he chooses. Lucas tells people on purpose because he knows how much it turns me on.

He sets his wineglass down and kisses me deeply. I moan against his mouth. Oh yeah, he's soooo getting some tonight.

Lucas murmurs between kisses. "After I told him about the con..."

He trails his mouth down to my neck. A tingle of delight ripples through me as he sucks and bites gently before he continues. "He offered his services if I was ever looking for someone local."

He must have really hit it off with Brian. I've fucked plenty of guys with big cocks, but it would be just like Lucas to give a friend a shot at me without being massive. Lucas is kind like that. Brian better give me a good orgasm, though.

"Mmm, so when am I fucking him?"

Lucas rubs my bottom lip with his thumb. "Well, the thing is, Brian likes to work in pairs."

My eyes widen.

Um, two guys? No, I've got to be wrong. I shake my head to clear my confusion and laugh. "Shit, I almost thought you meant he was bringing a friend. You want to be in the room?"

The way we do it, Lucas hides in the office. He listens through the adjoining wall while I fuck in the spare room.

Lucas grins in response. "No, you had it right the first time. He's bringing a friend, and I'm going to be listening in, like usual."

My brain freezes for a moment. When it kicks back on, a splash of wetness leaks into my panties and my nipples harden painfully. "You've arranged for TWO guys to fuck me?"

I keep thinking Lucas can't possibly surprise me, but he's taken the cake with this one. I never considered he'd want two guys to fuck me in one night.

He slides his hand into mine and squeezes it. "Yes, Brian and Damien. Only if you want it, baby. They are free tonight. Do you want two men as a Valentine's Day present?"

"Hell yes!" I answer quickly, and he chuckles.

"All right. Guess I should send out a text. Can you get the door when our food arrives?"

Shit, the food. My appetite evaporated when he mentioned two people were going to fuck me. Who needs food now? Oh wait, I need stamina.

"Sure, I got it."

He presses a kiss against my forehead. "Thanks, baby. I'm going to change my clothes and send the message."

My eyes glaze over as Lucas leaves the kitchen. What am I going to do with two guys? Hell, I'm going to have three cocks inside me tonight, since Lucas always fucks me afterwards.

Mmm... three cocks. Ms. Kitty buzzes her approval and I wiggle in my chair, trying to ease the growing ache. This Valentine's Day is shaping up to be a good one.

I bet I get at least three orgasms tonight. That's all I'm saying.

Chapter 2

The guys agree to come over in two hours, after we have dinner and I've showered and gotten ready. Since I'm not hungry, I pick at my dinner, moving the food around on my plate. At least I'm able to get enough down so Lucas doesn't complain.

We're both lost in thought while we eat, and it's good he didn't want to chat much. I'm way too busy daydreaming about two guys fucking me.

Are they going to tag team me? Like will one blow his load in my pussy and then let the other one have a go at me?

Ohhh.

Am I going to suck on one while the other fucks me?

The possibilities are endless.

Once I've eaten all I can, I push the plate away. "Love, I'm going to go take my shower. I can't eat another bite."

He winks at me in response. "Alright, baby. I'll take care of things here while you clean up."

Too excited to help, I blow him kisses and say, "Thanks, love," before heading to the bathroom. I let the shower water heat as I strip off my clothes. I pile my hair on top of my head in a loose bun; I don't have time to blow dry it this evening.

My mind wanders as I stand beneath the steaming hot shower. I rub the soapy loofah over my body and enjoy the vanilla scent of my body wash. Ms. Kitty was recently waxed, so I'm silky smooth in all the right places.

After my shower, I contemplate the contents of my lingerie drawer. If Lucas had given me more warning, I might have bought something new tonight. Fucking two strangers on Valentine's Day deserves a shopping trip. He didn't, giving me this delicious surprise, so I have to settle for something I already own. I tap my finger on my chin. Hmm... which item in my drawer says, "I'm a dirty slut who wants to take two men at once"?

I settle on a sheer lace lingerie teddy in red. The best thing about it? It's crotchless. They can bend me over and fuck me without removing it or ruining it. Plus, red seems appropriate for Valentine's Day.

Once I'm all put together, Lucas orders me to stay put in the spare room until he brings the guys in. He wants to have a little chat with Damien before the fun starts. This isn't my first rodeo, so I don't complain. It's how Lucas handles our casual flings.

Since there's two of them planning to fuck me, I feel extra slutty tonight. Hell, maybe I should be naked instead.

Nah.

I want to wear something feminine and festive. I stretch out on the bed and admire my reflection in the full-length mirror across the room. I'm like a sexy gift waiting for them to unwrap.

The doorbell rings. Since the spare room door isn't closed, I can hear murmured male voices down the hall. I'm a bundle of sexual energy while I wait. The guys must be single if they are free on Valentine's Day—wait, when did Lucas plan this? He didn't go to the gym this morning.

I don't have time to think about it because the guys head in this direction. Shit, it's go time. I peek into the mirror one last time to make sure I still look good.

Yep.

I smile seductively at them as they pause in the doorway, taking me in.

Damien and Brian are younger than I expect, maybe in their mid-twenties. They're tall and handsome with fit, muscular bodies. Oh fuck, it's been a while since I've had a young stud. Do I have the stamina to satisfy two younger guys? My pussy flutters at the thought of being used all night long by these two.

Yeah, we're willing to try.

"Hi guys," I deepen my voice to sound sexy and give them a little wave. "Come in."

Neither of them says anything as they jostle into the room. Do I make them tongue tied? Lucas is behind them and he stays in the doorway.

"Jessica, you okay?"

I nod. "Yes, I'm fine. I'll see you soon."

He closes the door. I wait a moment until I hear the soft click of the office door next to the spare room, giving him enough time to get settled into his usual chair.

Since neither guy has spoken yet, it seems I need to break the ice. "So, are you two ready to fuck me?"

Consider that ice broken.

They both laugh.

Brian replies, "Yeah, let's get this party started."

Mmmm, yes, let's.

Damien adds, "Sounds good to me too."

The guys strip quickly, and I'm glad I opted for the crotchless teddy. These eager guys might flip me over and use me. Shit, this is hotter than I expected. Two guys coming over here to fuck me and leave seems like the sluttiest thing I've ever done.

Their cocks bob slightly with every movement as they strip. I'm temporarily shocked at how enormous they are. I have a perfect view, and I can tell Ms. Kitty is going to get an incredible ride. My body hums with anticipation and my nipples tighten beneath the lace bodice. I'm too excited to wait and bring a hand up to tease one of my nipples.

Brian is undressed first and leans on the bed to kiss me. I respond to his gentle touch and the pressure of his mouth against mine by moaning. He leaves a trail of kisses along my neck and tenderly bites my earlobe. It's a good thing I'm lying down. My knees wouldn't hold me up right now.

When Damien takes a seat on the bed and starts rubbing my feet, I let out a blissful moan.

Fuck, I didn't know tonight came with a foot massage.

"Look at her tiny feet!" Damien comments.

What? Brian and I both glance down. My foot is so much smaller than Damien's hand. I'm not sure what they expected, as I'm quite petite, but maybe they hadn't noticed until now.

Brian laughs. "Shit, if that's how small her feet are, is she going to handle your cock?"

Me and Ms. Kitty perk up.

Damien's got a big cock compared to Brian? I'd looked, but maybe I needed to look again. Obviously, I missed something.

Oh. My. A tingle zings from between my legs and my pussy throbs. Oh yeah, we're so ready to get stuffed by an enormous cock.

The guys run their rough hands all over my body, caressing and kneading me. They're thorough, finding the small of my back, my thighs, my breasts, the sides of my neck. I close my eyes and let the sensations wash over me. My breathing quickens, and I am intensely aware of how hot and hungry they are for me.

Damien fondles my backside, and his voice is husky. "Fuck, Jessica, you look gorgeous in that lingerie. You have such beautiful breasts and an amazing ass."

Heck yeah! Tonight comes with compliments along with the foot massage? Score! I moan, "Thank you," as Damien runs a hand between my legs and rubs my pussy through the lace.

Brian whispers in my ear. "You know, we could do this while you're on your hands and knees."

Mmmm. I love being fucked from behind. He kisses my neck again and I murmur, "Whatever you want."

That makes Brian laugh. "Oh yeah, it is whatever we want tonight. Your husband said you were our little slut to use, and you enjoy being called filthy things."

I moan and bite my lip. "Yes."

Damien continues to rub my pussy while Brian explores my backside. I'm aching for a cock inside me, but their hands on me feel too good to make me want to hurry them along.

I lift my head to kiss Brian again and he groans into my mouth. "I can't wait to fuck you."

Ms. Kitty throbs. Shit, I don't know how long I'll last before I explode. Three orgasms is seeming likely.

Damien nudges me onto my back and then spreads my legs. The room spins a little as he slides a finger inside me. Why are they being so gentle? I gasp and arch my back off the bed when he massages my cave wall as pleasure radiates from my core.

"You're so wet, baby."

Oh, fuck. He used the pet name Lucas uses for me. I'm sure he didn't realize it since it's a common-enough pet name, but it still mentally fucks me up—well, that and the four hands all over me.

Brian plays with my nipples while Damien pushes a second finger into me. Ms. Kitty is a wet mess and I moan in bliss.

I don't know what to do with my hands, so I clutch at the comforter and try to hold on to some self-control. It's going to be hard not to scream when they fuck me tonight. Actually, Lucas would probably love to hear that.

Damien's fingers swirl around my entrance, making me gasp and shiver. "I think she's ready for us to fuck her."

I can feel my pussy throb with need. You can bet your ass I'm ready.

"I think she is too," Brian says. Damien pulls his fingers out of me, and I whimper. Damn it, I need a cock!

Brian kisses my neck and whispers in my ear, "I hope you're ready for his big cock."

"Yes, please." My voice is a murmur.

Mmm, I can't wait. Brian moves his mouth down to my breast. He runs his tongue over the lace on my nipple while I moan softly.

"Damien, I think this teddy is in our way. What do you think?"

Brian nips at my nipple. Damien responds. "Yeah, let's remove it."

Even though I'm comfortable in my skin, I'm still a little nervous about being naked in front of two people. Damien slides the teddy off my body, then they each grip one of my ankles, pulling my legs apart.

Oh, fuck. A wave of self-consciousness washes over me and I feel the urge to cover myself or turn off the lights.

Both men stare at me, and Damien's gaze lingers on my pussy. A trickle of moisture between my legs confirms what I already knew—I'm turned on. I become hyperaware of their every movement. It feels like they're drinking in my body with their eyes.

"You're gorgeous," Damien murmurs.

Brian says, "She's going to be a good little slut for us."

Damien laughs. "A slut who is going to get split open with two big cocks. She's so tiny, we're going to have to really jam in there to fit."

Fuck, that's filthy. I wish I could talk dirty back to them, but I'm tongue tied from lust, and I can't think.

Damien's finger strokes my pussy again, then he moves closer. I try to relax, but it's difficult. I'm wound up tight and ready to pop. My pussy throbs as Damien slides a finger inside me.

"You're so tight," he says as he finger fucks me, and delight pings my brain.

Brian moves to suck on the opposite nipple from earlier. His hot breath flutters across my sensitive skin and I groan.

"Mmm, so tasty," He murmurs. "We're going to stretch you out until we're balls deep in your little cunt. Do you want that?"

I whimper. "Yes, god... please."

"Such a good little slut." Brian latches onto my nipple and sucking hard enough that I gasp.

I love dirty talk. I already felt like a slut, but this drives me further into the mindset of being a slut. I'm about ready to let them do whatever they want to me.

Lucas better be able to hear this.

Damien rubs my clit again, and I moan. "Oh fuck, that feels so good."

He pushes another finger inside me, and finger fucks me roughly until I'm on the edge of exploding. I'm going to come all over his fingers if he keeps this up.

"Fuck, I need to be inside you, baby," Brian moans.

I get an illicit thrill whenever he calls me 'baby.' This is so fucking amazing.

I groan in protest when Damien pulls his fingers out of me. He rubs my clit with one hand while he lifts my leg up and presses the head of his cock against my wet entrance. They've been touching me and fondling for so long, I'm shocked that one of them is finally going to fuck me.

Jesus, it's about time.

"Are you ready?"

I groan and nod.

Damien grins and thrusts forward. Oh god, I can feel the tip of his cock stretching me open. It's so much bigger than Lucas's cock.

"Fuck," Damien moans. "We really might split her in half. She's such an itty bitty thing."

He's not wrong. My pussy feels stretched wide, and it hurts a little — a glorious hurt. I try to think about Lucas and relax my muscles. I've taken big cocks before, so I know it's going to feel wonderful once I adjust and he's buried balls deep inside me.

Brian kisses me again, and my tongue dances with his. My heart thuds in my chest in time with Brian's kisses and I swear I can hear it beating.

"You're so fucking sexy," he growls.

It feels naughty to be kissing a stranger while another stranger is shoving their massive cock inside me.

Brian keeps murmuring dirty things to me. "Your husband is going to love hearing us fuck you tonight. We're going to make you scream."

I groan, "Yes... yes," as Damien rocks his hips, sliding deeper inside me. I toss my head from side to side and writhe as he pushes in until he bottoms out. Jesus, it's such a delicious pain.

"Ohhhh, fuck," I cry out when he pulls out and slams back into me.

The headboard thumps against the wall with each thrust. I whimper and grip the comforter as he fucks me in quick strokes. Bliss radiates through me, and I can't think or do anything but hold on while he uses me. Moaning loudly, I put my feet flat on the bed and meet Damien's thrusts.

The room smells like sex mixed with my vanilla body wash and a hint of spicy cologne. The unfamiliar scent emphasizes how dirty this is. I may never see these two again. It's a wham-bam-thank-you-ma'am fuck. God, I love Lucas so much for arranging this.

Brian sucks on my tits again and the intense pleasure spirals me higher and higher. I'm mindless and insatiable. If I had known two guys would be this amazing, I would have begged for it months ago.

"Fuck, you're so wet and tight," Damien groans. "Your husband didn't tell us how tiny you are."

Damien whacks against me sharply and I cry out from the pleasurable pain. Quiet? I'm not being quiet now, so I know Lucas can hear, and I hope his cock is out. I imagine his hands moving up and down his length as he listens to my moans.

"Mmm, I bet she's never had two cocks at once."

Groaning loudly, I shake my head. "No, never."

I really want that. I want to suck on one of them while the other fucks me.

Damien pulls out completely and then slams back into me. "Are you ready to come?"

"God, yes."

He withdraws again and then slams home. I'm moaning continuously as he fucks me faster. I try to keep up with his rhythm, moving with him to match the intensity of his thrusts. I'm spiraling close to my orgasm as my pussy clenches around his cock.

"Fuck, I'm going to come," Damien moans. "I'm going to fill your little cunt with my cum."

Shit, I need to come before he does! He hammers into me frantically and his final slam skyrockets me into my orgasm.

"Ohhhhhh, fuck," I scream as a burst of pleasure shoots through my body.

Damien growls and jets of hot cum coat my inner walls. His cock pulsates and he moans. Ripples of delight continue to crash into me as Damien fucks me through my orgasm.

I don't notice when Brian stops sucking on my tits, so I'm surprised when he whispers in my ear. "You're such a good little slut. I can't wait to see how you look when we're done with you."

He kisses my neck and I shiver when he says, "Now it's my turn."

My brain is mush when the guys flip me over and pull me up onto my hands and knees. One of them rubs my ass and murmurs, "Such a pretty ass. Too bad Lucas said we can't fuck it."

Whaaa? Not that I want those monstrous cocks in my ass, but I didn't realize Lucas gave the guys instructions on what they couldn't do. I have such a wonderful husband.

Brian holds onto my waist. I arch my back and cry out as he slides his cock into me.

"Fuck, you're right. She's tight," Brian growls. "But she's gonna take every inch of this."

Brian grabs my hips and hammers into me. Sharp thrills run up and down my body. Fuck, this is amazing. I'm probably going to be sore tomorrow, but it's worth it.

"Mmm, you're so fucking hot," Brian moans. "I could fuck you all night long."

Damien moves in front of me on the bed and wags his cock at me. Fuck, he really is huge. That thing was inside me? Wait, how is he already hard again?

He holds his cock steady and aims for my lips. Um, he's expecting that to fit?

Brian gives a sharp thrust, forcing me forward. My gasp opens my mouth. Damien takes that as an invitation.

Ohh, fuck.

I have to open my mouth as wide as I can and stretch just to get the tip of him past my lips.

Yeah, there is no way I'm giving this dude a deep throat blowjob.

I study what I can see of his cock as I swirl my tongue around the head and suck on it. Prominent veins run up the length of his shaft. I taste myself on him, mixed with a manly essence that is all him. His breath hitches, so I can tell he's enjoying the suction of my mouth and the soft motion of my tongue.

Each time Brian thrusts into my pussy, it pushes me forward a bit onto Damien's cock. I have to hold myself steady while Damien slides his cock in and out of my lips, never fully withdrawing, while I suck like the greedy slut I am.

Damien reaches down and grabs my hair. "Fuck, your mouth feels so good."

I try to tell him I love sucking cock, but my words are muffled by his thick shaft in my mouth.

"You're such a good little slut," Brian pants. "You're going to make us both come really hard."

My moan is garbled. All I can do is hold on to the comforter while they use both my holes. My pussy is stretched wide and sensitive, and I can't think beyond the sensations coursing through me.

Damien groans, "Fuck, I'm going to come again."

He pulls out of my mouth, causing saliva to drip down my chin, and starts jerking his cock above my head.

"Tip your head up and stick out your tongue," he commands.

I close my eyes and do what he asks. Dammit, I really wanted to watch him come again, but with how enthusiastically Brian is fucking me, I'd probably end up with an eyeful of cum.

Damien groans and droplets of his warm cum splatter on my cheek and nose. One spurt actually lands on my tongue, and I swirl the salty goodness around my mouth before swallowing.

Yummy.

Once he's done showering me with his cum, Damien presses my shoulders down to the bed. I lower my head. What the heck is he doing?

The new position sets Brian off and he furiously pounds into me. Oh shit, he was just helping his buddy.

The erotic slapping of skin is louder than I expect as Brian's balls whack against my clit in this position. It's a sensation overload. My toes curl as my body shakes.

Oooh, god, I'm going to come! My brain is reeling, and liquid fire scorches through my veins as the tension inside me explodes.

I scream as convulsive waves grip me. My mind splinters as I get lost in my climax. Pleasure ripples through me in a tumbling wave as Brian's fingers dig into my hips and he comes with a roar.

He keeps slamming into me, filling me with his warm cum, while I shiver from the aftershocks of my intense orgasm.

When he finally pulls out, I collapse onto the bed, face down and ass up. Both guys are quiet for a few moments, and I drift in a blissful haze.

"Um, is she okay?"

Hands touch my cheek and I crack open one eye and try to smile at them. My mouth is half buried into the comforter, but I'm loud enough to be heard. "I'm fine."

I want to say, "Don't mind me, you just fucked me senseless," but that's too much work.

Damien strokes my hair and tells Brian, "I think you should go find Lucas."

The door opens and I assume Brian leaves. Damien keeps touching my hair and his voice is soft. "Are you really okay? We weren't too rough? Lucas said you wanted rough."

He sounds concerned, so I force myself to be more coherent and lift my head. "Oh god, that was amazing. I'm more than fine."

I can tell I've eased his concerns when he laughs softly. "Jessica, you're something else. I'm never going to forget this."

Yeah, I'm not sure I'm ever going to forget his cock, but I keep that to myself.

Lucas and Brian come back into the room. When I look at Lucas, I can see the tension ease from his face.

"Hi love!" I'm floating on cloud nine and giddy from my orgasm, almost to the point of sounding loopy.

Lucas chuckles. "She's fine guys. You just did a good job."

I hear fabric rustling, like Brian and Damien are getting dressed, but my focus is solely on Lucas. I crave being near him, assuring myself that our connection remains strong. Lucas sits on the bed and gathers me into his arms, kissing me passionately.

When he pulls away from the kiss, he laughs, using his hand to wipe drops of cum from my face. His hard cock presses against me as he whispers in my ear, "I'm going to say goodbye to them, then come back and make you mine."

I'm happy as I nod at him.

He kisses my nose and I settle back onto the bed. The men converse as my thoughts drift. I've seen some huge cocks, but Damien's was definitely the most impressive I'd experienced so far. I always think some guy is the biggest ever, as if I forgot the size of all the previous cocks, but this time I really think it is. If I had seen it in advance, I might have called off the whole night. That thing is intimidating.

Ms. Kitty gives a soft pulse in protest, and I chuckle to myself. Wait, who am I kidding? Ms. Kitty would have been begging to scale that flagpole.

I sigh in contentment and relax some more. Lucas needs to hurry back before I drift off completely.

Chapter 3

I'm lying on my side with my eyes shut when Lucas returns.

"Baby, you awake?"

I slowly open my eyes and smile at him. "Yes, I was thinking about you."

"You're stunning." He kisses my forehead.

I giggle in response. "Uh, thanks, but I'm kind of a mess right now."

He climbs onto the bed behind me and nuzzles my neck. "You smell like sex—it's hot."

My face lights up in a grin and I roll onto my back. "Well, I got used pretty good."

His hand cups my cheek and he looks into my eyes. "That's because you're a sexy little slut."

I giggle. "I'm *your* sexy little slut."

He kisses me and I run my fingers through his hair. We hold each other for a few moments, reveling in the warmth of our embrace, but soon the need for more becomes too great to ignore.

"Lucas," I whisper.

He kisses my cheek before pulling away and settling himself above me. He pushes his shorts down and our hips meet as his length presses against my entrance. His voice is deep and husky when he speaks. "Yes?"

"I want you to make love to me. Please, fuck me."

He kisses me tenderly as he slides into me. His thrusts are gentle yet intense, sending delightful pings through my entire body.

I grab his ass and urge him on. "More, please!"

He increases the speed and power behind each thrust, and I wrap my legs around him as he becomes the primal version of my husband.

"Did those cocks feel good?" he groans in my ear.

"Yes," I gasp out.

"Tell me how they felt."

"Big... hard... heavenly."

He thrusts faster, and my muscles around him tighten. I hold on to him, pulling him deeper as he pistons vigorously. I cry out as a soothing wave of pleasure washes over me. This orgasm isn't as intense as the prior ones, but the gentle bliss is a perfect ending for the night.

Lucas comes a moment later and groans with release. His body tenses and convulses as he pours himself deep into my pussy. He moves in and out a few more times before easing out completely and melting into my embrace. My pussy flutters from aftershocks of my orgasm and I almost giggle.

Oh yeah. Ms. Kitty is going to need a day of rest after this.

I'm not sure how long we stay cocooned together, but eventually Lucas shifts to lie beside me.

"Wow," I whisper.

He kisses my shoulder and sighs in contentment. "That was incredible."

I smile and snuggle up to him. "I love you so much. You've given me the best Valentine's Day ever."

"You're very welcome, baby." he murmurs.

My eyes droop, but a thought pops into my head and wakes me up. I steal a glance at him, and his eyes are shut.

"Hey, Lucas?"

I nudge him gently until his eyes flutter open. "Hmmm?"

He's looking sleepy and adorable. I could squeeze him in my arms and smother him with kisses.

Right. I was asking him a question.

I poke his stomach. "When did you plan all of this?"

He smiles as I question him and kisses my shoulder again. "A few weeks ago. I didn't tell you in case you couldn't finish your book. You might have been too busy daydreaming about being fucked by two guys with enormous cocks."

I erupt in laughter. Oh, shit. He's probably right. "Yeah, that was a good call."

He snuggles closer to me, laying his head on my breast as I run my fingers through his hair. I'm so damn happy. I don't think life can get any better than this.

The End

About Lacey Cross

I'm mainly a writer who got bored during the pandemic and turned to erotica out of desperation. I found out I love the creativity and challenge of self-publishing sexy stories. I write a variety of kinks, but most are wife sharing with a touch of BDSM power control.

Connect with me at:
  https://lacey-cross.com/

Acknowledgments

This bundle was another one of mine that took a small village to write.

Thank you Adam Gaffen for making my first editing experience by someone other than my regular editor painless.

Thank you Wordcat, for our help with Shared Hotwife at the Con and Sharing His Eager Hotwife. You know how much I appreciate everything you!

Thank you to my numerous beta readers who helped me with plot points (con details, haunted hause issues, etc). You all rock.

www.ingramcontent.com/pod-product-compliance
Lightning Source LLC
Chambersburg PA
CBHW031002210726
48290CB00007B/2428